ONCE A THIEF

BOOKS BY JAN THOMPSON

Protector Sweethearts (6 Books)
JanThompson.com/protector

Defender Sweethearts (6 Books)
JanThompson.com/defender

Binary Hackers (4 Books)
JanThompson.com/binary

Seaside Chapel (6 Books)
JanThompson.com/seaside

Savannah Sweethearts (11 Books)
JanThompson.com/savannah

Vacation Sweethearts (8 Books)
JanThompson.com/vacation

Keep up with Jan Thompson's book news:
JanThompson.com/newsletter

ONCE A THIEF

PROTECTOR SWEETHEARTS
BOOK 1

JAN THOMPSON

GEORGIA
PRESS

Once a Thief (Protector Sweethearts Book 1)

To my Lord and Savior, Jesus Christ, who died on the cross to save me from my sins and rose again from the grave to give me eternal life in heaven.

For God so loved the world that He gave His only begotten Son, that whoever believes in Him should not perish but have everlasting life.
—John 3:16

ABOUT PROTECTOR SWEETHEARTS
CHRISTIAN ROMANTIC SUSPENSE

From *USA Today* bestselling author Jan Thompson comes the Protector Sweethearts series of books that showcase Private Investigator Helen Hu and her associates and friends. This collection is a spinoff of Jan's **Savannah Sweethearts** and **Vacation Sweethearts** series.

Protector Sweethearts

- Book 1: Once a Thief
- Book 2: Once a Hero
- Book 3: Once a Spy
- (More Books to Come)

Protector Sweethearts
JanThompson.com/protector

For book release news, subscribe to Jan Thompson's
mailing list:
JanThompson.com/newsletter

ABOUT ONCE A THIEF
PROTECTOR SWEETHEARTS BOOK 1

She sets a thief to catch a thief.
Will he also steal her heart?

Private investigator Helen Hu must team up with reformed art thief Reuben Costa to rescue her mother, who has vanished while trying to make amends for stealing some bejeweled eggs connected to the Amber Room.

Reuben's Record...

To protect the woman he loves whom he cannot have because she is another man's wife, Frederico Costa goes to prison and leaves his art theft crime organization to his only son, Reuben.

When his father dies in prison, Reuben vows to never love or marry. He pours the next several years into expanding his father's activities across Europe, all the while sacrificing his own personal happiness.

Some years into Reuben's incarceration, the FBI Art Crime Team and INTERPOL offer him an early release from prison and a second chance for a new life in Greece if he helps them to catch a bigger criminal. Reuben agrees, and is now a free man.

Until they require his services again. This time, he must visit his own family's past in order to help private investigator Helen Hu find her missing mother and twelve Petros eggs, keys to the lost Amber Room.

Helen's Havoc...

Past memories have never been darker for Private Investigator Helen Hu as she deals with a long-lost secret that her mother has hidden from their family for fifteen years. Afraid that it will shame her daughter, Mama Hu tries to fix what she has done and redeem herself. Unfortunately, as Helen fears, she disappears.

The best way for Helen to rescue her mother is to go underground where thieves and robbers live. Her only ticket into that nefarious world is another art thief. He says he is reformed. Is he, really?

As Helen and Reuben rush to rescue Mama Hu before the matriarch gets herself killed, the unlikely partners end up bargaining for not only life and death but also their own hearts and souls.

Once a Thief is book 1 in *USA Today* bestselling author Jan Thompson's **Protector Sweethearts** Christian romantic suspense series featuring Private Investigator Helen Hu and her associates as they hunt for lost treasures, search for missing people, and defend noble causes.

In This Story World...

The events in *Once a Thief* happen after these stories, where Helen Hu makes several appearances. In fact, *Tell You Soon* is where we first meet Mama Hu.

- Tell You Soon (Savannah Sweethearts Book 2)
- Love You Always (Savannah Sweethearts Book 6)
- Reach for Me (Vacation Sweethearts Book 2)
- Share with Me (Seaside Chapel Book 1)
- Step with Me (Seaside Chapel Book 2)

Once a Thief can be read on its own without your having previously read any of the above books from Jan's contemporary Christian beach romance collections.

Once a Thief (Protector Sweethearts Book 1)
JanThompson.com/oncethief

Protector Sweethearts
JanThompson.com/protector

Subscribe to Jan Thompson's mailing list:
JanThompson.com/newsletter

ONCE A THIEF

CHAPTER ONE

A plunge away from the Aegean Sea, the town of Oia hugged the Santorini cliffs of the caldera, a haunting reminder of a volcanic past ever present in Helen Hu's mind as she parked the ATV and set off on foot down the pedestrian walkway.

Her company-issued iPhone told her where to go through the mishmash of cliffside buildings and tourist-packed lanes meandering around painted fences, containers of brightly colored flowers, and tiny blue hotel pools. The pastel-colored buildings looked like interlocking Lego blocks glued to the side of the rocky mountain.

Every now and then, Helen spotted blue domes, mushroom caps reaching toward the afternoon Mediterranean sky, portending bright days ahead.

Not!

The signal grew stronger. Helen spotted her mom in the crowd.

Mom was way ahead but slowing down now as she pretended to weave in and out of souvenir shops, stopping to touch a postcard or two, as if to leave fingerprints in case something happened to her.

What, Mom? What?

Swept into a wave of tourists and their multilingual tour guides, Helen quickened her steps across the uneven lanes sandwiched among shops and restaurants, villas and guest houses, private properties and potted bougainvilleas—all the while trying to keep an eye on Mom.

Mom had a distinct walk. Helen could spot her a mile away, always in one of her many identical pairs of five-inch-heeled jacquard boots. Those boots added inches to the diminutive woman and brought Mom to about Helen's height.

And those boots slowed Mom down enough for Helen to catch up to her in the crowded lanes and paths.

Helen suspected Mom wasn't here on Santorini on a quick weekend getaway—without her signature luggage when she had gotten off the ferry from Athens an hour ago.

So what is she here for?

Mom had made no attempt to hide. Her fuchsia blouse was bold and matched some of the flowering plants contrasting the surrounding white and blue architecture.

Every now and then, Mom would glance back, as if searching for something, looking for someone.

Meeting someone?

Helen looked away, just in case Mom spotted her. Even at sixty-eight, Mom's eyesight was way better than Helen's. And she had often said that she could identify either one of her daughters from miles away.

Helen wasn't about to test that now.

Not after all the trouble she had taken to get here. The notification had arrived while she had been in the middle of hunting down a fugitive passing through Frankfurt.

While Helen's Hu Knows, Inc., private investigative firm specialized in recovering lost art and missing persons, the company had grown and expanded into tracking down fugitives—since the day they had successfully helped the FBI apprehend an international terrorist who had abducted Helen's mom and sister.

Her sister had gone on to marry and have kids. But Mom.

Mom had retreated into her own little world after that episode.

Sometimes Helen wished that Mom would be more forthcoming with her. Since Dad had passed away so many years ago, Mom had tried to carry on with her life in fits and starts. As the years had gone by, she had withdrawn more and more into the recesses of her own thoughts and memories.

And now? Was this a part of Mom's multiyear introspection?

Helen felt a burden to care for her mom. At thirty-four years old and with no prospects of marrying and having children, Helen felt that she had more time than her sister to take care of Mom. In fact, Mom was already living with her back in Savannah.

Helen wouldn't mind if Mom lived with her the rest of her life. She wanted Mom to know that her daughters really wanted the best for her and that it was time for Mom to be transparent.

Yeah, right.

Helen pushed through the crowd toward Mom, as more people swarmed around Helen, down the steps and narrow walkways, looking for balconies to park themselves and set up video cameras and smartphones for their sunset viewing.

Sunset would be in two hours.

When Dad had been alive, they had come here often during summer vacations, only to see the sunset and to cruise on the Aegean Sea. Dad had been quite a yachting enthusiast. Helen and her sister, Sabine, hadn't taken to the water as much as Dad and Mom had. Sometimes their parents would take their own vacation.

The two of them would end up in Santorini— also known as Thira—or they'd sail to Crete, across the water, where they would stay in a villa owned by an old family friend.

Helen stopped.

Her iPhone signal showed that Mom had been inside that souvenir shop for over a minute.

Helen held her breath and ran, her black boots pounding the cobblestones beneath, the summer sun above her baking her baseball cap and shoulders.

Before Helen reached the souvenir shop, she heard the noise of a motor overhead. A drone in the sky hovered.

Someone taking photos?

She heard a popping sound.

Then another.

And another.

Pop! Pop! Pop!

Someone screamed, and the crowd went berserk.

The racket of screams and shrieks turned into a stampede as the tourists scattered like ants in the narrow lanes, any way they could to get out of the bottleneck, pushing and shoving Helen and everyone else in their paths.

Children and babies crying, people jumping over the low fences into hotel pools, people falling down as they were mowed over by shoes and knees and a mob gone wild.

Helen elbowed her way toward a low iron gate, thinking she could climb over it to safety.

Before she could get there, something whizzed past her ear—

And she went flying to the ground, sacked like a quarterback, sandwiched between the dirty cobblestone-and-cement lane and someone on top of her.

All around her were hot wafts of stinky shoes from the maddening crowd, the odor of sweat and fear—

And a sudden, distinct, clean smell of fresh soap.

"Get off me!" Helen's elbows and torso twisted this way and that to get the man off her back. She almost hit him with her iPhone, which was still in her grip.

He barely moved.

"Get off me!" she repeated, thinking he couldn't hear her in the concert of loud and chaotic footfalls.

"Shhh. It's still above." His voice was calm. Accented.

And definitely male.

The summer sun continued to beat down on them. The man's weight pushed Helen's backpack against her spine, probably crushing her iPad and magazine inside.

Police sirens blared in the distance, and the drone sounds eased away.

"We have to get out of here," the man said.

"Then get off me!"

As soon as the man eased off her, Helen wiggled out from underneath him as quickly as she could, her right hand reaching into her waistline pistol pouch—

"Helen!"

She heard the familiar sharp tone above the roar of the crowd.

She looked up, squinting in the shifting sunlight and shadows. She realized then that her sunglasses had been knocked off her face. "Mom?"

Mom tapped the ground with her boots. "What in the world are you doing here?"

Instead of giving Helen a hand, Mom leaned toward the man who had rolled off Helen.

He was trying to get up. He clutched his chest. "What sharp objects do you have in that backpack?"

"You okay?" Mom asked.

Helen scooted back against the gate to prevent herself from getting kicked by the rushing crowd.

"I think I'm okay." She brushed dirt and grime off her clothes.

"Not you. I meant him." Mom picked some grass off the man's hair. "I see you two have met—or shall I say, made contact."

Helen's eyes widened. "Please tell me you're not dating a man half your—"

"No, no. He's not my type. In fact, I think he's more your type."

"Mom!" Helen rose to her feet too quickly. The world swirled around her.

But strong arms caught her before she fell.

She smelled a whiff of clean, fresh soap again.

Male cologne.

CHAPTER TWO

"Eggs, Mom. You stole three Petros eggs." Helen Hu wanted to shake Mom's shoulders, but she looked too frail, too fragile, as she sat in the same seat that the Hellenic Police officer had told her not to move from some thirty minutes ago.

After the commotion in Oia—which was still under investigation—INTERPOL and the local Hellenic Police had led them to this safe house in the neighboring town of Fira.

They were still on Santorini because they had to wait for morning and the next available ferry to take them all back to Athens. They had missed the night ferry since the debriefing had gone on for hours.

Helen paced on the wooden floor, passing by Mr. Clean Soap on the sofa. They had been quickly introduced, but Helen had no interest in any of Mom's friends—especially friends from her less-than-stellar past.

Reuben Costa was stretched out on the sofa, asleep. It was past midnight, and beds were down the hall. He could have gone there. Why stay here? Why fall asleep here?

She thought he shivered a bit under the swirling fan. Like a puppy dog. Poor thing.

As soon as Helen had arrived in Fira, she had texted her offices in Savannah and Brussels to get more data on Reuben Costa. It was still daytime in the United States. In Brussels, Hugo never slept.

Hugo responded from the Brussels office, saying that he had called their friend, Camden La Salle. Camden had recently been reinstated as an FBI special agent. Because of his extensive work in Brussels and Frankfurt on art crime theft in the last several years as a private investigator, Camden had been able to get a position on the Art Crime Team in Europe. He would know more about the Costa family.

Helen herself had heard something in passing, but the Costas had been out of business for at least five or six years. Fifteen minutes after Hugo had texted her, he texted again with as much information as Helen could process at this late hour of night, tired from traveling and running and being shot at.

Who had shot at them?

Was it at her? Helen doubted it.

Hellenic Police was investigating, of course. It could take days or weeks before they found out what was going on with the drone, and whether it had anything to do with the case.

But Costa.

Frederico Costa had died in prison. Reuben Costa, his only son, had served time. It had been cut short when he had cooperated with the FBI and INTERPOL.

And now Mom had dragged the poor man back into the past.

It was strange that Mom had never mentioned her connections to the Costas until now.

Helen saw Reuben shiver again.

She picked up her backpack nearby and dug for her thin travel blanket she had stashed in the front pocket. She spread it over Reuben.

As the blanket landed softly on him, his eyes opened. "Thank you."

Helen nodded.

Behind her, Mom was saying something, but Helen only caught the last bit.

"...long time ago."

Helen turned toward Mom, as if an explanation was needed.

There was nothing more to explain.

The deed had been done.

Mom is a thief!

"Fifteen years... Not a long time, Mom."

"I should've told you when you took over Hu Knows, but I thought... Never mind. It's all over now." Mom sniffled. "Ondrej has died. I'm the only one left who knows what really happened when Fred and I broke into that museum in Athens."

Fred?

Ah. Yes. Frederico Costa.

Reuben's father.

As she sat by the empty table, Mom looked awfully small and worn out.

The secret she had hidden for fifteen years had now returned to extract another pound of flesh from her and carve more crow's feet onto her face.

What sort of guilt had Mom been carrying for so long?

You know, other than breaking into a museum and stealing eggs...

CHAPTER THREE

"You didn't tell Dad." It was partly a reiteration and partly a question.

"I told you that he died before I had the chance." Mom sniffled.

Oh dear.

Helen wanted to rush to her, to hold Mom in her arms, to tell her she would fix everything.

No. Only God could fix everything.

Still, Helen felt a heavy burden to salvage the reputation of Hu Knows, Inc., the family business her parents had worked so hard to build, from its inception as Hu Private Investigations to its renaming to Hu Knows, Inc., after Dad had passed away.

Well, Helen's only sibling didn't want any of

the company, preferring to go into real estate. Sabine had sold her share back to Mom, who had then left the daily operations to Helen.

All these years of hard work could be gone because Mom had kept thirty-million-dollars' worth of bejeweled eggs in someone else's safe deposit box in a bank in Venice.

Didn't she realize that Venice was sinking?

A door nearby opened and shut, and INTERPOL agent Damiano Kolovos stepped into the room, followed by a Hellenic Police officer who was carrying what looked like a steel briefcase.

"There's been a change of plans," Kolovos said. "Agents from the FBI Art Crime Team have arrived in Athens. They want to talk to Mrs. Hu. They don't want to wait for us to take the ferry. They offered to buy plane tickets."

"We'll get there in fifty minutes instead of five hours," Helen said. "All the better."

Officer Giannopoulos sat down across the table from Mom and put on a pair of gloves.

Other Hellenic Police officers and INTERPOL agents had been alerted to the exchange since the moment Mom had walked into the INTERPOL National Central Bureau in Athens with her fifteen-year-old tale that hardly anyone could believe.

Helen wondered why Mom hadn't gone to the FBI instead of INTERPOL.

Then again, this was Mom. Helen had stopped being surprised at anything Mom dragged in.

Whenever they had a minute, Mom would fill Helen in on what it was all about. While these eggs were not as famous or spectacular as the Fabergé eggs, Mom said that every egg collector knew the Petros eggs were somehow connected to the long-lost original Amber Room that had been taken by the Nazis in World War II.

Fifteen years ago, Mom, Frederico, and Ondrej had somehow stolen and hidden three Petros eggs out of twelve. Supposedly, the other nine were still scattered among anonymous private collectors across Europe.

Now, it seemed that someone was actively collecting all twelve eggs. If the puzzle eggs were opened, they would reveal twelve missing panels from the Amber Room, and more importantly, where to find them.

Even with just twelve panels, their sale in the black market could make the seller extremely wealthy the rest of his or her life.

Mom wouldn't have said anything the rest of her life had her retired partner in crime not passed away under mysterious circumstances in Thessaloniki a week ago. The box had been delivered posthumously.

A sign? A message?

All three eggs had been in pristine condition.

"Technically, Ondrej and I rescued the eggs from a criminal." Mom glanced at Giannopoulos, now putting on gloves and preparing a device to remove the microchip from Mom's hand.

"You mean a fellow thief," Helen corrected her.

"That's in the past."

"And then you delivered them to yet another criminal, who would probably sell the eggs to the highest bidder."

"That's INTERPOL's idea. They want to see who ends up with the eggs, and if they have the rest of the collection."

"You're going to jail, Mom." Helen wanted to be angry and upset, but what good would that do?

"What else do you want me to do? I've confessed everything to that Greek god—ah, male model—here." Mom pointed to Kolovos. "Agent K, may I call you Damiano?"

The fifty-something Kolovos—too young for Mom—neither smiled back nor responded.

Giannopoulos pointed to a spot on the table. "Madam, please put your hand here."

"Will it hurt?" Mom winced already.

"Just an ant bite. We're going to remove the microchip since we don't need it anymore."

I don't want to see this.

Helen turned away, walking toward the other end of the room, where the shutters covered the night sky outside.

Out there, Mom's enemies waited, having arisen from the ashen days of light and shadow, of chases down cobblestone paths, and of relics from the seventeenth century.

Relics.

Including the pocket watches that Dad had given to Mom, Helen, and Sabine before he passed away. If not for Mom's pocket watch, Helen wouldn't have known that she had been in Santorini unannounced.

She heard a click.

"Ouch," Mom said. "It hurts!"

"Just for a little bit," Kolovos said, standing behind Giannopoulos.

"Like how long is this little bit?"

"A couple of hours. Don't touch it. Keep the plaster on."

Helen turned around just as Giannopoulos applied a Band-Aid on Mom's wrist. "You'll be fine by the time we get on the plane."

"Before or after breakfast?" Mom's voice turned

sweet.

"We'll bring you something to eat if you're hungry."

"You'll eat with me, Agent K?"

Oh boy.

"No, madam. I have work to do. We need to follow the eggs while you go to your arraignment in Athens."

"What if they find the trackers inside the eggs?" Mom asked.

"They won't. We used NSA and British SIS technology," Kolovos said, as if he had to defend anything.

Helen didn't say a word, but she knew people who could get around those things. Besides, hadn't they just destroyed three antique eggs by messing with them?

She wasn't sure the eggs were still worth thirty million dollars.

Mom flexed her hand, the manicure in shades of orange coral sparkly on her fingernails under the fluorescent ceiling light. "What if I walk away?"

"Mom!" Helen couldn't believe what she had heard her say.

"You don't want to spend any more time in jail than you need to, do you?" Kolovos's voice was calm. He had probably heard worse from criminals.

Criminals.

So ashamed.

Helen wondered what Dad would say had he been alive today. Their whole family, including Mom, had worked hard to continue the private investigative firm. The FBI and INTERPOL had trusted them.

And now this blight from the past could ruin them all.

CHAPTER FOUR

W hen Helen Hu's eyes flared at him as she paced back and forth in the room, Reuben Costa had never seen dark-brown eyes more intense when angry.

Ah, emotions.

Emotions had been Reuben's own downfall.

When his father had died in prison, Reuben had been so distraught that he couldn't work for weeks.

Then he swung back with a gale force into the work his father had left behind. He had kept only those people loyal to his father, and in the name of Frederico Costa, Reuben had scoured all of Europe looking for the most expensive artwork, paintings, sculptures, and jewels.

Unfortunately, three years of nonstop thievery had done him in.

Bitter and burned out, he had made one mistake while living in the shadows of the night.

One mistake: trusting a woman.

As his father had done.

For the next five years, he had whiled away his time in that Barcelona prison, contemplating why his father would give up everything for a woman he could never have. Mama Hu, someone else's wife, had not reciprocated his father's affections. Yet Frederico Costa had shamelessly pursued her.

It had to be in her eyes.

The same eyes that her daughter had inherited.

When they look at you, you cease to exist.

Reuben tried not to blink as Helen Hu stared at him now, her eyes boring into him, killing him softly...

No. He could take her on. He could be different from his father and avoid falling into the traps of a siren, such as this woman's mother had been.

Like father, like son?

No. I will not look into her fiery eyes.

Fiery eyes.

Fiery?

Reuben had not met a fiery woman in five

years. Then again, it had been impossible to meet a woman without a criminal record, not in an all-male prison in Barcelona.

Ah, but I'm out now.

Reuben sat quietly on the sofa, with nothing better to do than to listen to the tap-tap-tap of Helen's black boots on the tiled floor. Every now and then she stopped in front of him, stared, sighed, and strutted away to the other end of the room.

She was an enigma. A puzzle.

Only hours before, she had loaned him her travel blanket.

Now she was shooting darts at him with her eyes.

It wasn't his fault that Mama Hu was in big trouble. That woman tumbled into the soup herself.

Still, it was amusing to watch Helen react to the entire situation.

Beyond where Helen had been pacing, the sparsely furnished room elongated toward a couple of tables pushed up against a wall. There, a trio of one-way rectangular windows showcased the early morning Santorini skies.

Reuben wondered if Helen or Mama Hu had gotten any sleep.

Speaking of Mama Hu, INTERPOL agents and Hellenic Police officers had taken Mama Hu somewhere else to give her further instructions. The delivery of the three bejeweled Petros eggs had been a success, but there was no telling what would come next.

Since Mama Hu and her daughter were both American citizens, INTERPOL had contacted the FBI Art Crime Team. Special agents from their bureau in Rome would be waiting for them in Athens sometime today.

Athens.

Where Reuben had seen Mama Hu for the first time in fifteen years. She had shown up unannounced last week, offering to clear his father's name of the murder charge.

An art thief Father had been, but not a murderer.

Yet, Father had been tried, convicted, and sent to prison for a murder of passion.

He had died in prison, so what good was clearing his name now?

Then again, Reuben had to do this for Father's memory.

Somehow he had to make it all work out. Mama Hu had gotten herself into a tangled mess.

Of all people, Reuben knew how to unravel it. How to fix it.

Reuben had helped the FBI Art Crime Team

before. That had been how his imprisonment had been reduced to five years.

There was no way now that he would do anything to jeopardize his freedom.

This was Mama Hu's penance, her grief, her sin.

Not his.

"Why are they taking so long with Mom?" Helen's voice was tinged with worry.

Reuben knew how it felt to lose a parent. In his case, his father. He had no memories of his mother, and thus hadn't missed her at all.

"She could get herself killed." Helen paced again.

"I told her." Reuben uncrossed his legs. "I told her the moment she came to see me last week. I'm a free man now. I don't want trouble."

"But she didn't listen." Helen sighed.

Reuben wasn't sure how to respond to that. If Helen had relationship trouble with her mother, there was no reason for him to get involved. A stranger merely passing through, Reuben only wanted to clear his father's name.

A piece of cake, right?

Except this piece of cake had poison in it.

Helen stood at the window. Tapped the pane.

"Ballistic," Reuben offered as he joined Helen

at the window. Greeting his eyes was a panorama of more whitewashed buildings of Cycladic design, dropping away into the blue ocean.

Sometimes he wondered what was underneath all that water. Was Atlantis really down there? What about treasures—

Ah, those were the days.

Today he was a simple man.

Pushing thirty-eight, he was happy to lead an uncluttered life. Better easy and free, than complicated and incarcerated, no?

Working as a landscaper for his landlady in Athens suited Reuben just fine. She had given him a discount for his studio flat, and had provided him with all the tools he needed to carry on the business her late husband had started.

That was, until Mama Hu had appeared at his flat and shown him a photograph of three Petros eggs. Dazzling and bejeweled, they had been hidden away for fifteen years. Now they were worth untold millions in the black market.

And there were nine more of those.

A dozen eggs. Keys to the original Amber Room —or at least, parts of it.

Mama Hu had asked Reuben to go with her to the INTERPOL National Center Bureau in

Athens, where they would meet someone she knew.

"Your mother wants to make things right," Reuben explained to Helen.

"You said it like you don't believe it." Helen's voice was almost a whisper.

Reuben didn't respond.

"I think there's something you haven't told me." Her eyes met his.

In the early morning sunlight, Helen's eyes were not as dark brown as he had thought. The fire had ceased, and in its place was liquid tranquility.

Reuben could see speckles of gold in her eyes.

Gold?

In the glowing light, Helen's features were part Asian and part...

European.

And those ethereal lips...

Her lips reminded Reuben of an old photograph of Mama Hu, the only one in his father's safe deposit box in the Zurich bank, right next to a lady's diamond bracelet of dubious origins.

There had been nothing else in the safe deposit box.

"It's not polite to stare," Helen said.

Reuben snapped out of his memory bank.

He gazed into the great and marvelous

outdoors. Seabirds flew by. In the distance, an airplane left streaks in the sky. Little puffy clouds floated here and there. The entire scenery looked like it came out of a children's storybook.

"My mother can be chatty," Helen continued. "She must've done something, said something to convince you to leave your clean life and return underground, where it's dark and dirty, where you could lose your freedom again if you misstep."

"We're working with INTERPOL. It's all legit. Besides, it's over. The eggs have been delivered. We can all go home now."

"Do you think that's all?"

"Isn't it?"

"My mother is unpredictable," Helen said. "She broke up with her latest boyfriend two months ago and has been looking for something useful to do."

"Too much information."

"I want you to know where Mom is coming from."

Reuben felt warm fingers on his arm. Then they were gone, as if she had done it without thinking and then changed her mind.

"This mystery about those Petros eggs..." Helen took a deep breath. "I wonder if Mom is trying to relive her past, back in the days when she and Dad roamed Europe, looking for cases to solve. They were building their PI business."

"So you think it was all business?" It was premature for Reuben to tell Helen about Father's infatuation with Mama Hu. And how they had met long before Mama Hu had married someone else.

And then fifteen years ago, Father had met with Mama Hu again. They had also attended their mutual friend's funeral. The deceased had been run over by a bus while trying to cross a busy street in Thessaloniki.

"Look—I'm not trying to defend Mom." Helen waved her hands about.

"You would see your mother in jail?"

"I will visit her." Helen's voice cracked.

She seemed to misunderstand what Reuben had tried to say, but he let it pass.

"Thieves go to jail. That's all there is to it." Helen bowed her head. "Dad worked so hard to build our PI company, and now I find out Mom is a thief."

"Was a thief."

"Once a thief, always a thief." Helen walked to the other end of the room, sat down, and didn't speak to Reuben again that day.

CHAPTER FIVE

Their flight from Santorini to Athens was short and sweet, no more than fifty minutes. If they had taken a ferry, it would have cost them five to six hours of traveling time.

Kolovos and Giannopoulos sat on both sides of Mom. Helen sat separately at the back of the plane, since she had to pay separately for her own ticket.

The only person missing aboard the flight was Reuben Costa, who had completed his role of accompanying Mom to the meeting place, when Mom had handed over three Petros eggs to her brokers.

The brokers were probably en route now to

deliver the eggs to the buyers. Those buyers were on INTERPOL and FBI radar.

Every now and then, Helen was curious about who those buyers were. She wondered if they were anyone from Mom's past. Mom had been tight-lipped about disclosing any more than the INTERPOL had asked her.

Then again, it wasn't Helen's problem.

She had only shown up in Santorini because Mom's tracker had gone off.

The rest of today would be spent retaining the best defense attorney Helen could find for Mom. After that, Helen would have to go back to work pursuing fugitives. She might go to the Brussels office to catch up on what she had missed the day before, if anything.

At the airport, Helen picked up her carry-on at one of the luggage storage facilities on-site. She was glad it was still there because she didn't have time to buy new clothes and toiletries.

The Hellenic Police van taking Mom away to downtown Athens didn't wait for Helen. Mom was gone by the time Helen signed for her compact Fiat Punto rental car.

In fact, if Mom hadn't approached the INTERPOL National Central Bureau in Athens—housed inside the Greek Police Headquarters—

about the three Petros eggs in her possession, Mom's life wouldn't be in danger either.

At a red light on the way to the ancient city of Athens, Helen was on the phone with Camden La Salle. He was in Zurich. He didn't say why.

"I can't help you, Helen. I'm sorry. If I were on the outside..."

"I hear you. Thanks anyway." Disappointed that Camden couldn't disclose information that the FBI Art Crime Team had, Helen knew she couldn't pester him and get him into trouble.

"On the other hand, if you find anything, be sure to let us know," Camden said.

"Right. Will do, Cam." Working with the FBI often meant it didn't go both ways. The FBI Art Crime Team was inundated with old unsolved cases. Searching for the nine of twelve missing eggs wasn't their top priority.

After all, these were not Fabergé eggs.

Then again, her mother's life was more important than any of these things.

Helen reached for the coffee in the cupholder only to find it empty. She leaned back against the driver's seat, willing herself not to fall asleep.

She prayed for God's mercy upon her family. All the hard work Dad had poured into the company could come to an end if the Hu family had been complicit in a crime all those years ago.

As the bearer of the Hu name, Helen did not want to hear of any bad news.

As a private investigator, she wanted to know where the other nine Petros eggs were.

Did Mom have any more eggs stashed away somewhere?

Traffic slowed to a standstill due to some sort of commotion ahead. Helen turned on the radio to see if there was a traffic report, but it was all in Greek. She googled and found no information.

She tapped the steering wheel as the car inched forward a little at a time. She heard sirens in the distance, and prayed for whoever were involved in the apparent traffic accident ahead.

Gray smoke rose into the sky. Horns blared.

At the accident site, Helen saw firefighters dousing water over a smoking van. Partially charred sides told her that the van had caught fire—

The van looked familiar.

Unmarked, it looked like the same van that had taken Mom.

Helen pulled off to the side of the road, jumped out, and ran toward the van. A police officer stopped her from getting closer. On the road, a large piece of cloth covered a body. Nearby, someone groaning on the ground was being treated by emergency medical personnel.

She skirted the area to get closer to the man on the ground. When they lifted him onto the cot, she saw that it was INTERPOL agent Damiano Kolovos. Badly injured and bleeding from one leg.

"Mom?" As Helen stood behind the tape, her eyes searched for any sign of Mom. Nowhere in the crowd of police and paramedic uniforms.

Nowhere.

Helen swallowed.

They took Mom.

CHAPTER SIX

It had been three hours since Mom had gone missing, a long time indeed, and Helen's team in Savannah and Brussels had worked tirelessly to track Mom down. Helen found it hard to coordinate from a long distance, so she instructed Hugo to pack up and fly to Athens to join them.

Helen made more phone calls and found a safe house outside Athens with a secure internet connection, courtesy of the Central Intelligence Agency, who also wanted a piece of the pie.

Apparently, the FBI hadn't found a need to inform the CIA of their egg hunt with INTERPOL.

Art theft yielded funds that had to go some-where. Therein was the connection. The CIA had been investigating a possible money flow between art thieves and terrorists at large. Every terrorist activity had to be funded somehow.

With various law enforcement agencies cracking down on the usual sources of funding, terrorists had to get creative.

"Like which terrorists?" Helen asked.

At the other end of the phone, Dario de la Cruz didn't answer her directly. "Tell me why you need a safe house."

When Helen mentioned Frederico Costa, Dario went quite silent.

Then he wanted to know what Helen knew about the Costa family, and that was her clue that the CIA thought there was a connection between the Costas and the people the CIA were most interested in.

Mom hadn't spoken much about the Costas all these years. Their name had only surfaced since Helen had been in Santorini.

Helen had no opportunity to talk to Reuben about his family. Somehow Helen didn't think Reuben wanted to go back to his old job. It only led to one place: prison. Still, she had only met him less than twenty-four hours ago.

She wanted to ask questions, but Dario had to go. Something more urgent called his attention.

Once again, information only flowed one way: to the federal government.

Still, Helen now had leverage: one missing grandmother and twelve missing Petros eggs.

Whoopee.

While Helen wouldn't put it past Mom to orchestrate her own escape, she didn't believe that Mom would have caused any deaths.

At least not intentionally.

And certainly not law enforcement officers.

Altogether, two Hellenic Police officers had died: Giannopoulos and the driver of the police van. INTERPOL agent Kolovos was in the hospital.

Only one person was unaccounted for: Eleanora Hu.

Mom.

Mom's pocket watch had been found in the police van. It must have fallen off Mom's pocket in some sort of struggle. The homing beacon was useless now, sitting in the Hellenic Police station for safekeeping.

What had happened?

Helen went to the hospital to talk to Kolovos, but he was in surgery, fighting for his life. In the waiting room, she ran into a couple of special agents from the FBI Art Crime Team. They, too, wanted to talk to Kolovos.

Before she left the hospital, Helen called the Hu Knows, Inc., branch office in Brussels.

Then she called Camden La Salle again in the privacy of her Fiat rental car to ask him to find a way to retrieve Mom's pocket watch.

His response startled her.

"Stay away, Helen. Let INTERPOL and the Hellenic Police deal with this."

"And the FBI." Helen kept her voice low, but she was getting angrier by the minute at being an outsider.

"Yes, an American citizen is missing. We're on it. Trust me."

"I want to, Cam. We've been in many operations together, but this is my mom we're talking about."

"And twelve missing Petros eggs. This cannot end well—no, I mean, don't worry," Camden said. "I'll keep you appraised."

"Don't call me. I'll call you. Is that it?" Helen's heart sank to the bottom of the Fiat floor.

She said goodbye, hung up the phone, and drove out of town, back to the Eleftherios Venizelos International Airport to pick up Hugo. Dario would arrive separately. He had to wait for his computer specialist to reach his office in Rome before they could fly out together to Athens.

Helen entered the airport terminal and walked toward the baggage claim—her second trip in twelve hours.

She was on time.

But the carousel was empty.

She checked her messages.

Oh.

The three-hour flight from Brussels had been delayed by an hour.

Helen lifted her eyes to the summer skies. "Lord, are you teaching me patience?"

CHAPTER SEVEN

The midnight air sweeping across the ferry was freeing and refreshing to Reuben Costa. His dark wavy hair stirred in the wind, then rested again. He felt the breeze on his scalp.

Real sea breeze.

When he had been in that Barcelona prison, the salty taste of freedom and the smell of the ocean had often visited his memory bank. Those thoughts and remembrances had kept him going for four years, until one day in his fifth year, when a fellow inmate told him about freedom for his soul.

Eternal freedom is found only in Jesus Christ.

The question of his salvation—or lack thereof—

had bothered him weeks after that encounter with a criminal who had believed in Jesus while in prison.

If he could, I could too.

Lord Jesus, will you save me?

And He did.

Reuben smiled to himself as the passenger beside him got up and left the bench on the open deck of the ferry. He placed his shopping bag on one end of the bench and stretched out his entire body on the seat.

The soft blanket inside his canvas bag provided a semi-comfortable pillow.

Helen had given him the travel blanket.

He didn't know why.

Perhaps she had thought that he needed it more. Perhaps she didn't want it back now that an ex-prisoner had touched it.

Whatever.

He'd take any gift of comfort.

Across from his bench, two people were chatting away in Greek, one of the five languages that Reuben spoke.

"Yeah. Around nine-thirty this morning," he said. "A police van collided with another vehicle. A key witness was abducted."

Witness abducted?

Reuben's thoughts immediately went to

Mama Hu.

Wasn't her flight supposed to arrive in Athens around nine o'clock?

Reuben waved to them. Speaking in Greek, he asked what the news was.

"You haven't heard?" The man came over. He showed Reuben his smartphone. The news was on.

"Wow. You can see the news on this thing?" Reuben asked.

The man gave him a where-have-you-been look. He turned the sound up.

With a brewing headache, Reuben watched the entire news clip.

A Hellenic Police officer had been bludgeoned to death and dumped on the side of the freeway going out of Athens. Another police officer and an INTERPOL agent were shot. The officer had died on the way to the hospital.

An elderly woman was missing.

At the end of the news clip, there was a phone number for anyone with information to call. Mama Hu's photograph was plastered on the small screen.

"They're tweeting this and sending it out on social media," the fellow traveler added. "There's a manhunt on."

"She's an old lady who might be ill or something," his traveling companion added. "There's bound to be a reward."

Reward? I don't care about that.

The only person Reuben thought of when he saw Mama Hu's photo was Helen.

I must go to her.

But how?

"How much does one of these things cost?" Reuben returned the smartphone to its owner.

"You can get it for cheap these days." He named the lowest price in euros.

"I can afford that."

"You cannot *not* afford it," the man said. "Do you see any pay phones anywhere in Athens?"

"No. You have a good point."

"Also, how are you going to text your girlfriend if you don't have a phone?" He winked at his traveling companion, who chuckled.

Reuben felt like he had missed out on something.

You know, like keeping up with technology.

He had to. He had no choice. Technology was being used to track those Petros eggs.

If they hadn't removed the microchip from Mama Hu's hand, they might also be able to track her.

Technology would have allowed Reuben to call Helen right now, to ask her how she was doing.

He almost knew the answer.

She wasn't doing well if Mama Hu was missing.

Reuben closed his eyes.

As much as he had harbored animosity toward Mama Hu—even when she had come to him, pleading for help—he would not wish for Helen to suffer a loss.

The loss of Reuben's only parent had marred the rest of his life and outlook on living.

Reuben would like to think that Father had died of a broken heart, his love spurned by a married woman whom he had secretly admired, helped, and had taken the fall for.

Yes. Frederico Costa had gone to prison for a crime he had not committed.

To protect a woman he had loved from a distance.

The woman who had now been abducted.

And who has two daughters who would miss her.

One of the daughters looked like she might not be completely Asian, after all.

A scary thought.

Please, Lord, don't let us be related. My life is bad enough, as it is.

CHAPTER EIGHT

A plate of spanakopita for his lunch was all Reuben had asked for in the small café outside his temporary home. Having arrived in the morning after an overnight ferry ride from Santorini, he had taken the bus from the terminal to his rental flat, greeted his landlady, and then taken a nap.

By the time he awoke, it was past two o'clock in the afternoon.

After the late lunch, he went to a local electronics shop to find the cheapest smartphone he could afford. Then he walked home to charge up the battery and read the small print in the instruction manual.

A few hours later, on a wooden bench under a

tree in a courtyard, he tried to bash two things together: the manual and the phone.

Busy pushing buttons he didn't understand, it had taken a while for Reuben to notice that a shadow had settled in front of him.

He looked up.

And was surprised to see her.

Helen Hu.

"I need your help, Reuben. How much do you charge per hour?"

Reuben pointed to the other end of the bench. "Please do sit."

"I don't have time."

"You need a breather."

"I don't have time to..."

"Breathe?" Reuben patted the bench again. "Exactly. Two minutes and we'll go find your mom, okay? In fact, that was why I bought this phone. I was trying to text you."

"You don't have my number."

"Actually, I do. Your mom gave it to me."

"But you didn't have a phone."

"I still don't, at this time. I'm about to hurl this into the trash can." He almost meant it. Perhaps technology wasn't for him. He usually left those kinds of things to paid employees who worked for Father.

"Shall we see what we can salvage?" Helen opened her palm out.

"It's in Greek."

"To you?" She laughed.

"It's really in Greek." At the corner of his eye, Reuben spotted a black car drive by beyond the low brick fence and black wrought-iron gates.

"Oh. Switch to English, please? I'm illiterate in Greek."

Reuben did as Helen asked, and handed over the phone and manual to Helen. The manual had several languages on it. Regardless of the language, Reuben couldn't set up his phone.

"You don't have Wi-Fi," Helen said. "What you wanted to set up requires it."

"Why what?"

Helen rolled her eyes. "You also don't have enough bandwidth to download anything."

"What does that mean?"

"It means you can only use this phone as a dumb phone."

"Dumb?" Reuben laughed. Then he spotted another black car drive by. It seemed to be the same size as the first one a couple of minutes ago.

"To make phone calls," Helen said. "That's all you can do."

"What about sending messages?"

"Says here that texting will cost you money."

"No wonder the phone was cheap. The plan was cheap too. I guess I didn't realize there were add-ons." He packed away the phone. "I'll return it to the shop."

"How do you make phone calls, then?"

Reuben didn't answer. He looked past Helen toward the gate and brick wall. Through the gate, he could see the vehicle's side.

It's that black car again.

This time the car slowed down. Something glinted through the window.

"Get down!" Reuben yanked Helen's hand. They both went down on the ground.

He pointed to the back door of the apartment complex. "Can you get to the door?"

"Crawling?" Helen pointed to her skirt.

Why on earth would she be wearing a skirt today?

"You'll skin your knees on the concrete floor." He heard two car doors open and shut.

"Run!" He grabbed Helen's hand, and they rushed toward the building door, heads down, almost duck-walking, just as shots rang out.

Pushing Helen into the house, Reuben slammed the door shut and locked it.

"Whoa. What was that?" Helen followed him down the dark hallway.

"I don't know. But we have to get out of here." He reached for the keys to his landlady's car. His landscaping lorry didn't have the power to outrun a car.

"Did anyone follow you?" Reuben asked as they ran down the steps on the other side of the building, toward a busy street where the landlady's car was parked.

"Not sure."

"Not paying attention?"

"I'm usually not followed."

"So it could be me then." He unlocked the car door. "They could be coming after me."

Helen climbed in. "Why?"

"That's what I want to know."

They buckled in and sped off.

In the rearview mirror, Reuben saw two men coming out of the back of the building. He had no idea who they were or what they wanted.

The black car came up behind the men, and they climbed in.

"God help us," Reuben muttered as he merged into traffic, trying to get away from the black car now coming after them.

Helen glanced back. She probably saw the same thing. "Who are they?"

"I'm not sure I want to find out."

Helen was on her phone when Reuben turned a corner. "We go to the police station."

She nodded. Texted and nodded again.

"Who are you sending a message to?" Reuben asked.

"Why? Do you have to know?"

"Please tell me you called the police." Reuben waited for an answer.

"I sent out an SOS." She paused. "You'll need to call your landlady when we get to the police station. She could report a missing car."

"Yeah." Reuben tried to change lanes. Traffic was getting heavy.

Not being used to driving around town except in his landscaping lorry—which followed a regular route—he now made a wrong turn. The police station was in the opposite direction.

"Let's see..." Helen tapped her phone several times. "Nearest police station."

"Your phone can do that?"

"It's only a map." Helen shrugged. "We still have to follow instructions."

As if on cue, the map program spoke. "Make a U-turn as soon as you can."

Reuben heard the phone loudly and clearly. "I'm trying!"

A car swerved in front of him.

Reuben slammed on the brakes. He looked in the rearview mirror and spotted the black car coming toward them at a high speed.

Before Reuben could tell Helen to get out of their car, the black car rammed them.

The airbags deployed.

CHAPTER NINE

Cuts and abrasions on their faces and arms notwithstanding, Helen and Reuben made it to the safe house outside Athens without another incident.

A nurse had been waiting for them. Other than those bumps and bruises, both of them had been declared fit for duty.

Helen's liaison in the CIA, Dario de la Cruz, had shown up in person, validating their shadow team.

After a hot bath, Helen ambled downstairs with her iPad. When she reached the spacious library-turned-operational-center, all eyes were on her.

The new shadow team was forming, and if they

didn't tread carefully, they would be in a world of hurt.

Hugo, her faithful employee who had gone everywhere she sent him—and still hadn't quit on her—was on the phone. Helen heard him give instructions to Earl, who was at the Savannah office.

Helen made a note to herself to give Hugo a pay raise or offer him the director position of her European office, wherever she ended up planting it.

At the other end of the table was Leland Yang-Joule, a hacker that Helen had borrowed from the NSA by way of the CIA via Dario. It didn't matter to Helen how she came about it. The CIA would pay Leland's fees, but for this week only, she would be assigned to this operation to find a connection between Dario's terrorist and Helen's art thieves.

"Alive and well. Good to see you." Dario waved from the coffeemaker on a side cabinet by a wall.

There was a mirror hanging over the side cabinet, reminding everyone that this was a vacation home or a private villa. They were only passing through.

The quicker, the better.

Helen sat down in one of two empty chairs next to each other. She swiped her iPad. "Where's Reuben?"

Against Dario's better judgment, Helen had insisted that Reuben be a part of their problem-solving team. She knew Dario was probably tracking and watching Reuben. That was fine with her. In fact, Helen could not expect anything less from the thorough Dario.

"Coming." Reuben's voice echoed in the stair-well and reached Helen, whose back was facing the hallway.

He sat down next to Helen.

Her senses heightened.

He smelled clean and fresh.

Just the way I like—

Helen cleared her throat.

She hardly knew Reuben.

Yet, she knew a lot about him, his past, his present, his connections to Mom.

Speaking of connections...

"It's time to link the dots," Helen said.

What would be Reuben's dot or dots? Helen wondered if she could trust him. Was she prejudiced against his background?

Somewhere in his portfolio, it had stated that he turned religious in his last year in jail. He had given a written testimony of having accepted Jesus Christ in his heart. His fellow inmates had agreed that he was a changed man.

Are we not new in Christ?

Helen glanced at the clean-shaven, neat-and-tidy man sitting next to her.

He did not look like a thief.

A slight smile accentuated his dimple.

Mom would approve.

Mom!

Right. We need her home.

"Our purpose tonight is to connect every dot we have and let Leland's program find a way to extrapolate the connection. The goal here is to find Mom ASAP."

Everyone nodded.

"Too bad Cam can't be here," Hugo said. "He'd be a useful addition."

"Dario knows enough about the Petros eggs." Helen waited for Dario to say something.

He didn't.

"We begin a week before Santorini," Helen said.

"Or fifteen years ago," Reuben said quietly.

Helen placed her hand on Reuben's arm—before she realized she was doing it.

"Ah, let's do. Why don't you fill us in on it?" Helen said.

Reuben tapped the pen on the notepad in front of him, then sat back. "Fifteen years ago, my father fell in love with Person A. Some of us thought that might have been Mama Hu, but it's all speculation based on circumstantial evidence. Her photo was in his safe deposit box. However, in the same box was a diamond bracelet. In my one week of interaction with Mama Hu, I realized that she doesn't wear diamonds."

"No," Helen said. "Mom prefers something gaudy, colorful, and loud."

"Like her multicolored jacquard boots."

"Exactly." Helen nodded. "Also, Mom is a talker. She lives with me, and she talks my ears off. However, I have never once heard her mention Frederico Costa. It was always Edgar this, Edgar that. Edgar was my dad's name."

"Something is off, but we don't know what it is," Dario said. "I'll look into it, if you want."

"Will you? That will be terrific," Reuben said.

Leland raised her hand. "From what I see to this point, your bad dudes are techno-savvy. They sent a drone to follow Mama Hu in Oia, even after the egg exchange."

"Did they? Why would the drone shoot at Mama Hu if they wanted her alive?" Hugo asked.

"We don't know if it was shooting at her," Helen said.

"Right. That's under investigation," Dario

added. "Meanwhile, we might also consider that they had put a tracker on Mama Hu during the delivery."

"Which could explain why they knew when she would arrive in Athens." Helen thought for a minute. "Then again, anyone could check the flight schedule or use conventional surveillance means."

"On the drive to Athens, who dared to kill two police officers and wound an INTERPOL agent—and then abduct the witness?" Hugo talked as he jotted something on his iPad.

"Who has Mama Hu now and what for?" Reuben asked.

"Why don't any of her tracker and homing beacons work anymore?" Helen asked. "Where is she such that there are no signals out? A cave? Underground? Where?"

As soon as the meeting was over, Helen was on a secure line, calling Sabine in Savannah. She was seven months pregnant and obviously concerned about Mom.

"Tell me everything, Helen." Sabine's voice was controlled.

Deliberately, slowly, and sparingly, Helen

explained to her that Mom had disappeared about seventeen hours ago. Helen spared Sabine the gory details of a roadside abduction.

When Helen was done, Sabine was silent, and then she said something odd. "You mean like those Fabergé eggs? Enamel and gold?"

"It's not that popular or expensive."

"Whew. Good to know. Dad gave me a replica."

"What?" Helen sprang off her bed. She had come to her bedroom to lie down, to calm down, and then call Sabine.

Now she was sweating.

"He said if I kept it, then Mom won't get into trouble. I must've been about five years old."

"That long ago?" Helen counted in her head. "Twenty-seven years ago?"

"Uh-huh. I dropped it a bunch of times. It's all chipped up."

"Oh, I recall that now. You rolled it around your dollhouse."

"And I rolled it down the stairs, remember?" Sabine laughed. "It went clunk, clunk, clunk."

"Huh. Was it heavy?"

"I don't know. After Dad died, I put it in a safe deposit box together with the other things Dad bought me from his trips overseas."

"What other things?" Helen asked.

"You're not jealous, are you?"

"No, no. Mom is in danger. Maybe Dad left us some clues. Can Ming access your safe deposit box?"

"Yeah. It's in the bank downtown."

"Is Ming around?"

"We just had lunch. He's about to go back to work. Wait a sec." Sabine called for her husband.

While Helen waited, she thanked God for Dad.

Dad must have known Mom would get into a boatload of trouble. He had prepared the family. Maybe?

Helen repeated to her brother-in-law what she had told Sabine, but with more urgency.

"Ming, you need to get Sabine to a safe house. Then FaceTime me with the contents of the safe deposit box."

"You're looking for a chipped, cheap, chicken egg?"

Helen hung her head. "Okay, English major, go get your wife and kids to safety, and help us bring your mother-in-law home."

CHAPTER TEN

"We have to get some missing pieces before we can extrapolate some geo-location to track down Mom, considering that her signals are all lost," Helen said.

"We need names. Names are connected to people, places, things. Can you think of anything or anyone in the art underground who might want those eggs—assuming they were why Mama Hu is in danger?"

"So we go the old-fashioned way." Reuben smiled. It looked like he was trying to welcome them to his world.

"What's your mom's real name?" Leland asked, typing.

"Eleanora Hu nee Wu, also known as Mama Hu."

As soon as Helen said it, Hugo broke out laughing.

"Shut up, Hugo." Helen shot daggers with her eyes. It didn't work.

"I see now why Mama Hu doesn't use a hyphenated last name," Hugo carried on. "It would end up being Mama Wu-Hu. Woo-hoo! Get it?"

Nobody laughed.

Then Leland said, "You're so fired, Hugo."

"I'm sorry you think of funny things when Mom's life is on the line," Helen said quietly. "It has been over twenty-four hours. No news from the FBI or INTERPOL. It's up to our ragtag group here to find her. Have some decency."

Dario didn't wait for Hugo to apologize. "Molyneux."

Leland nodded.

There seemed to be more that the two hadn't said about Molyneux, but it wasn't the time for Helen to ask questions. She simply made a mental note to look up Molyneux, the terrorist at large.

Was she really getting investment capital from art thieves?

When no one else said anything, Reuben spoke. "My father's name was Frederico Costa. He has no nickname. His brother's name was Javier Costa. He fell off a boat and drowned several years ago."

"So sorry," Helen said.

"I don't feel any grief, really. He and my father had not spoken for years before my father died in prison under mysterious circumstances."

"Interesting." Leland continued typing. "Bad blood between the brothers?"

"No idea. Uncle Javier once loved a woman, but she died young."

"Find out the woman's name," Helen instructed Leland. "And Ondrej's last name. Mom kept mentioning him. He died suddenly last week. How all this began."

"Got it."

"What about your father's rivals?" Helen asked Reuben. "Was Ondrej a rival?"

"A friend, I think. But rivals? There are many." Reuben laughed. "Name any art thief, and he or she would be a Costa rival or enemy. Some have passed away, and some are still alive."

"This could grow our database." Leland rubbed her palms together. "Seed it with some more names, please."

"The top two that come to mind are Manolas,

Ioannidis..." Reuben paused. "There are more. Fairfield, Palmeiro."

"Are they people who are looking for the Petros eggs?"

"Ah, that rules out the Ioannidis organization. They don't care about eggs." Reuben seemed to be deep in thought. "I would move Palmeiro to the top of the list."

"Palmeiro? That sounds familiar. Wait a sec." Leland raised her eyebrows. "Searching for upcoming events tells me that they're hosting a ball this Friday."

Helen snapped her fingers. "If the list of guests is like the who's who of the art theft underworld, then some of them could have those last Petros eggs we want—or at least know of people who might."

Leland nodded. "But it's only three days away. Name someone we can send."

Slowly, Reuben raised his hand. "I'm the only one who will not raise suspicion."

"You could be a problem with our communication system," Helen said. "You're a Luddite."

"I can learn new tricks."

"We'll see."

Dario swiped his own iPhone. "It's a winner's ball. Meaning you need to bring a prize. Something you acquired—stole—that is more valuable than anything else you have at the moment. It has to be a thing, not a person."

"Ha." Helen shook her head. "So it's not going to be a kidnapping fest."

"What would be a valuable *thing*?"

"Easy." Helen leaned forward. "A Petros egg. What about museums out there? Do you think some of these might be displayed anywhere?"

"They haven't been in museums for a long time," Dario said. "But we have a master list of illegal private collections."

"It could take forever for us to scour private collections for one egg to bring."

"Seven years ago, Palmeiro had three," Reuben said. "However, he was robbed all the time. He might not have any left."

"And Mom had given up her three eggs so that INTERPOL can track them," Helen said.

"So they're starting to surface," Reuben said.

"You're suggesting...?" Helen asked.

"I go to the ball. Make a short list of people of interest."

"I don't think you should go alone," Dario said and Hugo concurred.

"No offense." Hugo saluted Reuben. "But we need a buddy system to protect the artifact."

"Then I go with him," Helen said.

Reuben smiled. "As my wife?"

"You wish."

CHAPTER ELEVEN

The shortest flight from Athens to Venice would take two and a half hours. They'd have to rent a ballroom gown for Helen and a tuxedo for Reuben. Helen had assigned Hugo to do all that.

Reuben hadn't worn a tuxedo in years. He wasn't sure if he could handle the memories of evening dinners in palatial dining halls, eating food he didn't care for, meeting Father's friends, who backstabbed him later.

Life in the underground was a bitter darkness of despair.

Why would he want to go back there?

To rescue Mama Hu.

If she was still alive.

After dinner, Reuben crossed the tiled hallway upstairs to his bedroom, hoping to read and rest.

He heard a door click.

Helen walked away from her room, holding an empty glass. It looked like she was heading to the kitchen to get a cup of water or juice.

"Helen?" Reuben said softly.

Helen stopped, then kept walking.

Reuben reached her. Stepped in front of her.

She lowered her chin.

"Helen?" Reuben lifted her chin.

Her eyes were red. Watery. Clearly she had been crying.

"Do you want me to get you a glass of water?" Reuben asked.

She nodded.

"Wait here." He took the glass from her.

He was back in no time with a bottle of cold spring water from the refrigerator downstairs. Helen was nowhere to be found.

Reuben knocked on her bedroom door.

She opened it. "Want to go sit on the rooftop terrace for a little bit?"

"Sure."

Five minutes later, she was pouring her heart out. "I want to believe that Mom is a survivor."

"I'm sure she is."

"That she'll find a way to live through it." Helen sipped the water. "We're grasping at straws sometimes. I thought that my sister's egg was one of the Petros eggs, but it turned out to be a child's-play replica made in China."

Reuben laughed. He uncapped his bottle of mineral water. "Any word from INTERPOL?"

"Not since Mom disappeared. Cam said that the FBI is only involved in a peripheral way since INTERPOL is in charge of this search-and-rescue mission."

"The CIA is on it."

"And then we're all over it. I fear there are too many cooks in the kitchen."

"You fear it would endanger your mother's life."

Helen drank her water slowly. "By noon tomorrow, she will have been gone for two days."

Reuben knew then that he wanted to make Helen happy again.

He knew what he had to do, even if it meant sacrificing his own freedom in the end.

He could talk to Dario about it. Perhaps the CIA would back him up.

Perhaps not.

But he had to do it, no matter how they responded.

For Helen.

He had seen how Helen and her mom had been close, back in Santorini. That flash of love between mother and daughter.

That bond.

A mother's love that was foreign to him.

He had to do this. Regardless.

His mind was made up.

And he would begin by calling some old friends. They would be surprised to hear from him, to learn he was returning to the business.

But it had to be done.

For Helen.

CHAPTER TWELVE

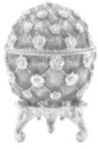

T he next morning, Helen awoke to an awfully quiet house. She padded down-stairs to a grandfather clock striking six thirty. She could hear Hugo snoring from one of the bedrooms downstairs.

She turned on the light in the kitchen and found the coffee carafe still hot.

Hmm...

Leland dragged herself into the kitchen, walked past Helen without a word, and poured the last drop of coffee into her mug.

"Did you get any sleep?" Helen asked.

"A few hours more than Reuben and Dario—" Leland stopped. "Oops."

"Have they left?"

"They've gone to look for eggs." Leland avoided Helen's gaze. "I'm sorry. I told them I wouldn't say anything."

"And you haven't. All we talked about was the lack of sleep some of us are getting."

"I do have a note for you." Leland dug around her pockets and fished out a wad of crumpled paper.

Helen flattened it out on the kitchen table. It was from Reuben.

"'I'll see you in Venice Friday late morning. We'll pick you up at the airport.'" She read the note aloud.

"They've gone ahead of me. Why not take me with them?" Helen made more coffee.

Leland seemed to be waiting for another cup.

"Anything more about Ondrej?" Helen asked.

"His death was unusual. He had lived in Thessaloniki most of his life. And then one day, he simply walked off the waterfront into the sea and drowned."

"Was he drunk?"

"His body was never found."

"Isn't that interesting? Two days later, his widow sent three eggs to your mom." Leland rehashed what they had already known.

"Assuming three was all he had."

"Exactly."

Helen sat down across from Leland at the kitchen table. "Suppose Ondrej had more than three Petros eggs..."

"Would he try to sell some of them in the black market?" Leland asked.

"Palmeiro would be all over it. Who else?"

"Costas."

"Reuben is the only Costa left." Helen sipped coffee. "His uncle also drowned in the ocean, supposedly."

"So many watery deaths."

"Speaking of the Petros eggs, have you tracked down the last known locations of those eggs?" Helen asked.

"Funny you should ask me that. They were scattered everywhere in Europe in the last twenty years."

"What's funny about that?" Helen got up from her seat. She peeked into the refrigerator to find something that looked like breakfast.

"Seven out of the twelve eggs showed up at the same time as the sightings of other lost pieces of artwork," Leland said.

"Like what kind of artwork?"

"Get this. Panels of the Amber Room that used to be in Catherine the Great's Winter Palace."

Helen nodded, remembering the information that Hugo had sent her only the day before. "It was begun in the early eighteenth century by the king of Prussia. About fifty years later, the entire room ended up in Russia as a state gift."

"Right. Then during World War II, Nazi Germany wanted the room back. The entire room. Imagine that."

"Wasn't it in 1943 or something?" Helen wasn't too clear on the history. It hadn't been something she had any interest in—only because no client had asked her to find the Amber Room.

The reproduction had been made, and the lost original panels seemed to have faded into the cobwebs of past history and folklore.

"Well, 1943 was the last time the Amber Room was ever shown to the world," Leland said.

"But in the seventies, pieces of it sold in the art underground."

Leland could barely contain her excitement. "Word is, Palmeiro and Frederico Costa had a bit of a sparring going on. Each trying to be the first to reconstruct at least one wall of the Amber Room."

"Palmeiro?"

"Apparently he has been looking for anything related to the Amber Room for the last forty-five years. He's ninety-three years old now, and informers told Dario that he had given up on the search."

"This is the same patriarch of his family of thieves who is hosting the ball tomorrow night."

"There is no family of thieves." Leland got up, poured herself another cup of coffee. "Palmeiro has outlived everyone in his family. He's the only one left."

"And he still hasn't found what he has been looking for all these years."

"Nope."

"How sad." Helen glanced at her pocket watch. It was still working. The mechanics were in shape. One couldn't tell that it had a homing beacon in it.

Helen returned the pocket watch into its place. She had kept it all these years.

She caught Leland before the hacker ran off. "You were going to show me something, remember?"

"Ah yes." Leland motioned for Helen to go with her.

"And this is why Dario called you."

"Right. INTERPOL borrowed the mini receivers from the SIS," Leland explained. "I'm familiar with them. The manual switches are not hard to activate."

"Only getting to them is." Helen sighed.

CHAPTER THIRTEEN

"Was your father protecting someone else?" Helen suddenly asked as they drove to the villa outside Venice for the ball.

They had rented a two-door Koenigsegg CCXR Trevita to fit in with Palmeiro's crowd, and that had burned a hole in Helen's budget. Since Reuben was more familiar with Italian roads, Helen had let him drive it.

Reuben had a feeling that Helen prayed he wouldn't scratch the car.

He wished that the CIA had paid for half their Venice excursion. However, it had turned out that Dario hadn't briefed his field office in Rome about this escapade, and they were too miffed to sponsor a car of any kind.

Reuben suspected that Dario was in big trouble, though the CIA had retroactively—albeit reluctantly—approved the pursuit of Palmeiro because they believed the money trail would lead them to the terrorists they wanted.

In the middle of this mess with Mama Hu, Helen wants to know about decisions my deceased father might have made?

"Why are you asking me such a question now?" Reuben asked.

"If that person is still alive, he or she might be in danger," Helen explained. "What about your biological mother?"

"I never knew her. My father raised me alone."

"Were you adopted?"

"I don't know."

"Have you considered looking for your biological mother, just to be sure?"

"No." Reuben knew his answer was curt, but it was the best he could give her.

This wasn't the time for her to dig into his past. At all.

Already, he felt bad about Thursday's series of antique picking with a trusted CIA sidekick by his side. Reuben knew he hadn't lost his ability to scale museums and steal jewels without being caught.

And that hadn't been what he had done on Thursday.

He had spent the entire night searching Palmeiro's estates for Mama Hu and the Petros eggs.

"All we got is a big goose egg," Dario had declared after fourteen hours of nothing.

So now they had driven to the ball without a prize to show.

They might not even be let in.

And Mama Hu would still be missing.

They had reached the sprawling villa. Reuben slowed down the sports car, waiting for the gate to open.

"Do you want to know the truth, Helen?" he asked. "I don't want to be involved in this mess at all, but your mom thinks it will clear my father's name."

Helen's shoulders sagged. "I would love to sit down with her and find out what she's been hiding all these years."

"Me too. She's the only link to my father."

"I hear you."

"I've left my life of crime. They've given me a second chance. I cannot go back. I dare not go back." Reuben eased into the slow procession of guests in their vehicles more expensive than this one. "I don't care about all these jewels or art pieces anymore. I don't want to go back to prison. I want to go to my tiny flat where the rent is paid for. I want to live my dull life in peace."

"My mother could wish for that very thing someday, when she sits behind bars and doesn't hear a bird sing."

Reuben reached for her hand. Held it warmly in his. "I am sorry. I didn't mean to..."

"I could say I would do anything to get my mother back, but I won't. I won't cross the line."

"I know you won't. I don't wish upon you a tainted past that haunts your future."

"It's not only that, Reuben. I have to give an account of my life to God."

"That too."

The valet parking was up ahead, but at the rate people got out of their vehicles, it would be a while before they got there.

Reuben had scared himself the day before when he had eased so easily into his old role.

"If they see that we don't have any artifacts or something with us, they won't let us in," Reuben said.

"I think they will."

"Why do you say so?" What did Helen know that Reuben didn't?

"If Palmeiro is holding Mom hostage, then we're just bonus," Helen said.

"If we end up in the same dungeons, I don't know if we can get out."

"Dario, Leland, and Hugo are on standby. Don't worry." She patted his hand.

CHAPTER FOURTEEN

J oseph Palmeiro himself greeted his guests inside the palatial Renaissance palazzo. Holding court in the grand ballroom under painted tray ceilings and walls lined with marble statues, Palmeiro shook gloved hands until he saw Helen and Reuben heading his way.

The smile evaporated from his face, and his jaw hung. He leaned heavily on his cane.

"You look like someone I know," Palmeiro said to Helen. "Your name?"

"Helen Hu." She did not extend her gloved hand to him.

A moment of recognition alighted on his face. "You were named after someone?"

"My grandmother."

"Is she still in Taiwan?" There was sadness on his face. "I haven't left this house in thirty years, except to go to church."

A thief goes to church...

So many things crossed Helen's mind.

Then again, God forgives. Redeems. Heals.

"Grandma? She passed away before I was born," Helen said. "How would you know about her?"

What is Palmeiro up to?

"Your mother?" he asked.

So many questions.

"My mother is missing."

Alarmed, Palmeiro's face changed. "What?"

"Someone abducted her in Athens on Friday. Something to do with the Petros eggs." Helen watched Palmeiro's face.

"Did you say Petros?" Palmeiro made a loud grunting noise. "She's worth more than all the Petros eggs in the world."

"You know my mother?" Helen wondered how. Mom had never mentioned him.

"It has taken me sixty-eight years of waiting." Palmeiro grunted again. "When we find her abductors, I will kill them, of course."

The way he said it, it sounded as nonchalant as, "I will drink tea, of course."

"Where have they taken her?" Palmeiro asked.

"We don't know. We're unable to track her. She could be anywhere." Helen tried to keep her voice even, but it was increasingly hard.

"Criminals!"

"Isn't everyone here a criminal?" Helen dared to ask.

"We're honorable criminals."

Is there such a thing?

"You tell me what happened to your mother and who you think is responsible," Palmeiro explained.

"We have no idea."

"Someone she knows?"

"Mom knows a lot of people. She has too many best friends. Talks entirely too much."

"Like her mother. Helena..." Palmeiro quietened. "Ah... So long ago."

"You do know my grandma."

"She was a tour guide in Florence. Seventy years ago."

Seventy years ago. Helen couldn't process the new information. "You didn't answer my question. How did you know my mom and grandma?"

Palmeiro's eyes were far away, as if going back in time. "Is your mother... Does trouble follow her like pollen on a spring day?"

"Oh yes." Helen's eyes widened.

"Like mother, like daughter." His eyes glistened.

"If you care for them at all..." Helen's breath caught. "Mom is still missing."

"What?" Palmeiro leaned toward Helen.

"I told you. They have Mom. Do you know who might want her?" Helen asked. "Or do you know who might be searching for those Petros eggs?"

"I don't have any Petros eggs. Not anymore," he said. "I stored five or six—I can't remember—of them in my vault. Someone robbed me while I was at church one Sunday a few years ago. I suspect that my butler did it, but I can't be sure. Can't get good help these days."

"Your butler?" Helen didn't know what to think.

"Well, yes, don't you have one?" Palmeiro asked.

"I DIY everything."

"DIY?"

"Do it yourself."

"Well, it's grammatically incorrect to say 'I *do it yourself* everything,' is it not?" Palmeiro asked.

Helen didn't want to argue with the nonagenarian, especially one who carried such a big stick in the art underworld.

It was becoming clear to her that whoever had tried to point at Palmeiro had an agenda.

Palmeiro was only the smoke screen.

"When I had those seven Petros eggs, it seemed prudent then to try to find the rest," Palmeiro said.

"You said earlier it might have been five or six eggs. Now you said seven."

"Well, Helen, it's been a while. I can't remember everything. All I know is that now I have zero eggs. I wasted forty, fifty years on all that. It's over for me."

"Someone wants to collect all twelve eggs. Why?" Helen asked.

"These are puzzle eggs," Palmeiro explained. "You'll see your treasure if you make it to the end. Or it will be the end of you before you make it. Either way, it's not worth the stress."

Not worth the stress.

Several people came to shake Palmeiro's hand, interrupting their conversation.

Helen was thirsty. "I'd like some water, please."

Palmeiro made eye contact with a server, and he came running.

The mineral water was refreshing, but Helen wanted to sit down now. Reuben seemed to sense the discomfort she felt.

"Perhaps we can sit down somewhere," he said.

"Yes, yes." Palmeiro led them to a settee.

On the way there, he turned to Reuben. "I knew your father. He was an honorable man, albeit with a poor judgement of women. You're doing better than he did."

"Thank you, I think."

"That woman was no good for him," Palmeiro added.

Helen gasped. *Not Mom!*

"I warned Frederico. That Agneta was keeping two beds warm, but he refused to listen."

What? Who?

Helen tugged Reuben's sleeves. He looked a bit shocked as well.

She felt that Mom had been vindicated.

"When Agneta passed away fifteen years ago, it was tragic. Such a senseless accident."

"Oh?"

"She was crossing the street to meet someone. Right in front of a bus." Palmeiro shook his head.

"Your father was devastated. Gave up on life. What's the lesson there, son?"

"Trust God alone?" Reuben offered.

"I was going to say that it's important to look to the right and left—and then right again—before you cross a busy road."

"That too."

CHAPTER FIFTEEN

Reuben skirted the waltzes and dances, leading Helen through the French doors to a small, uncrowded veranda outside. It overlooked a manicured courtyard of box hedges and fragrant fruit trees of several kinds. There were other people milling about by the unlit fireplace, but they soon left.

Reuben needed a moment with Helen, to assess her emotions. Remembering their Athens rooftop conversation, he wanted to be sure she had held it together.

Their unexpected meeting with her maternal grandmother's former boyfriend, and the subsequent hour-long interrogation to extract as much information as possible for Papa Palmeiro to beat up the criminals who had stolen his daughter—or who he had thought was his daughter—had ruined any hope of Reuben and Helen waltzing the night away.

The gravity of an abducted mother made every moment gray and funereal.

And the gravity of a life of crime made life itself an unbearable weight around one's neck.

Reuben recalled what Palmeiro had told them earlier this evening.

You'll see your treasure if you make it to the end.

Or it will be the end of you before you make it.

Either way, it's not worth the stress.

Reuben understood now what his own father had gone through all those years of chasing shadows down cobblestone paths in forgotten medieval and renaissance cities of old.

Relics.

Only relics.

There were other things more worthy of his pursuit. Like a beautiful smile on a pretty face.

Reuben ran a thumb across Helen's jawline. He felt the smoothness of her skin. He wasn't sure why he did that. The fact that Helen hadn't flinched or pulled away encouraged him to leave his thumb on her chin.

She looked at him, as if waiting to see what he was going to do.

Reuben thought that the cloud would part and the moon would shine and he would see her more clearly.

Instead, a bolt of thunder cracked in the distance, and rain fell like sheets in the courtyard.

Helen laughed.

"What? You read my mind?" Reuben asked.

"No need. It's written on your face."

"What is?"

"A moment you wanted. Lost."

"That so?"

In the rain, Reuben heard a door close. He leaned toward Helen. "Someone's coming. Play along."

His nose nuzzled her hair. He ran his fingers across the base of her neck.

She lifted her face toward him.

Is she expecting something?

Am I able to deliver?

Reuben kissed her softly on her forehead.

Then her cheek.

And lips.

Helen pressed against him. She didn't say a word.

He smiled as their lips met again.

"We seem to be…"

"Seem to be what?" A voice boomed in Reuben's ears.

Startled, he stepped back. The night was darker than he had anticipated. He had a hard time seeing in it, but he felt that someone was standing near them, watching them. If he had a flashlight…

A figure stepped forward.

Too familiar a figure.

"Uncle Javier?" Reuben drew a deep breath. "I thought you were dead."

"That's the idea."

"But…"

"I don't even care for boating."

"Who fell overboard?"

"A volunteer, obviously."

Helen reached for Reuben's hand. Held it tightly. Her palm felt sweaty.

"You're showing yourself in public after so many years," Reuben said. "Does Palmeiro know you're here?"

"You can ask him later when he comes around. In the morning, I think, after the sleeping pills wear off." Javier shrugged. "Even a ninety-three-year-old man cannot resist a woman offering him a drink."

"Why are you here, Uncle Javier?" Reuben asked.

"Thank you for still calling me uncle."

"I shouldn't after what you stole from my father."

"We were supposed to share Raphael and Picasso." Uncle Javier threw up his hands. "Enough talk about the dead. I saw you chatting with Palmeiro. I want to reconcile."

"It may never be possible now that Father is dead." Reuben tried to excuse himself and Helen, but Uncle Javier didn't move out of the way.

Several tall and too-muscular men surrounded Reuben and Helen.

"Take a walk with them." Uncle Javier pointed to the courtyard. "We'll stay in Venice tonight."

Somewhere beyond that was a carpark—a parking lot.

"In the rain?" Reuben asked.

"What's a little bit of rain?"

And thunder crackled again.

CHAPTER SIXTEEN

P ushed into the limousine, Helen and Reuben sat next to each other, thigh to thigh, holding hands tightly.

Ten blocks away, the vehicle turned into a tree-lined driveway that went for a long time until it came to stop at a porte cochère.

The door opened, and the bodyguards' hand-guns ushered them into the house, through grand hallways, and into a spacious parlor. There was a grand piano and several stringed instruments.

Holding court in what looked like a comfortable antique armchair, Uncle Javier eyed them both.

"Do you play any musical instrument?" Javier asked Helen.

"Poorly at the piano."

"You will play the Steinway. It's long unused. Gathering dust and all that."

Helen didn't respond.

Javier turned to Reuben. "I hope you took a nap today. It's going to be a very long night for you."

"What do you have in mind?"

"More Petros eggs."

"You! It was you." Reuben lurched forward.

The two armed bodyguards pushed him back violently.

"Don't break his ribs—not yet." Javier chuckled. "He still remembers how to be a thief. That's a skill long lost these days."

"I don't know where those eggs are," Reuben said.

"You don't, but I do. I know exactly where they all are. It will take you four days to gather all of them. My men will go with you."

"Helen goes with me too," Reuben said.

"No. She stays. She's insurance."

Reuben was about to say something, when Helen touched his sleeve.

Their bodyguard tried to separate them.

"One minute with my boyfriend?" Helen pleaded with Javier.

"All right. One minute!"

"A bit of privacy?" Helen asked.

"Talk here."

Helen leaned against Reuben and pressed her face against his shoulder. Then she raised her chin close enough to whisper in his ear. "You must return."

"I will." They were forehead to forehead. "I'll take you to dinner."

"Where?"

"I found a place in Fira."

"It's a date, then."

While they were talking, Helen slid her pocket watch into Reuben's tuxedo pocket.

He didn't react, but Helen was sure he felt the weight of something new.

"I'll miss you," she pressed her lips against his chin.

His eyes seemed to cloud over.

And he held her tightly.

Midnight came and went, but Helen couldn't sleep.

The guest bedroom was simple in its decoration, but the windows were covered with steel grids. The door was locked.

She was a prisoner here.

She had changed out of her ballroom gown into a sweatshirt and a pair of track pants that Uncle Javier had so graciously provided his guests.

Helen checked all four walls for panels and passages out of this rectangular room.

There was no way out.

The door, then.

The maid had left, having forgotten something.

Helen reached for the pins in her perfectly coiffured hair. She bent the pin slightly and began to pick the lock of the only door out of this bedroom.

The door clicked open.

Unfortunately, the only shoes she had brought with her were high-heeled shoes. The villa had provided her with slippers, but they were too big for her feet. They made flopping noises when she walked. In the end, she kicked them off.

Barefoot, Helen tried to remember where the stairs were. There were so many doors on this floor that the entire place looked like a puzzle box.

Gilded trims lined wall after wall, reminding Helen of the 1920s. After running around the hallway in circles and returning to where she had started, she began to wonder if this was an M. C. Escher nightmare.

She ran around it again, this time taking a

sudden turn down another hallway. It was dimly lit and foreboding.

At the end of the dusty hallway, gilded spiral stairs led down somewhere.

She felt like a bird in a golden cage as she climbed barefooted down the cool, steel steps.

Gradually, she could hear the piano.

Was it the same piano as in the parlor?

She nearly slipped down the last few treads, but landed safely in what looked like a massive library of old, unread books.

She checked all the doors. They were locked, except one.

She prayed for mercy from God.

Don't let this be a mouse trap.

Down the carpeted hallway was another flight of stairs. She went down those dark steps, as there was nowhere else for her to go.

She began to hear muted humming. And distant coughing.

Eighties music in between bouts of coughing.

She sounded like—

Mom.

Helen drew closer to the humming, which seemed to come from the other side of the wall. She tapped the wall in Morse code.

Someone tapped back.

Helen found a light switch and flicked it on. And searched the wall for buttons or an out-of-place panel.

She wasn't sure how long she was at it.

She felt someone standing behind her. She turned around slowly.

Rather tall and imposing, with a mop of short, cropped hair on top of his head, the guard carried a sidearm and walked with the gait of a weight-lifter. But his eyes were soft, as though he were looking for someone.

"I'm looking for my mother," Helen said.

"Everyone is looking for his mother." He laughed.

CHAPTER SEVENTEEN

It was a side of Mom that even Dad had probably not understood. Her need to test the darkness and taste its bitter fruits.

One could say it was even Edenic in nature.

Fatalistic, yes. Death often lurked and knocked on doors of those who sought after evil.

You ask for evil, and evil comes.

So why had Mom done it? Why had she tempted herself with a labor of sin and despair?

Was it pride that had led her to hide a double life?

Led by the now deceased Ondrej, the trio had focused on jewels. Most of their fortune had been spent by now, save for these Petros eggs.

Now the love of all things shiny had come to claim Mom.

The sounds of slamming doors outside this padded room echoed away into silence. Helen pounded the only door in the rectangular room. She inspected the wall.

It was of no use. There was no escaping this place.

Someone had to open the door from the outside to let them out of this golden cage that the body-guard had locked them in.

Helen found herself sitting on the floor, her shoulders against a wallpapered wall, her arms cradling Mom's head on her lap.

"We need to get you out of here and to a doctor." Helen stroked Mom's hair.

Mom was coughing more. Helen guessed that Mom had probably fallen ill sometime this week.

Surrounding them were printouts, pencils, blank pieces of paper, and crumpled trash paper spewing out of trash cans.

The rest of the small room was filled by a white Formica table and a couple of chairs. On top of the table were twelve Petros eggs in a carton, including the three from their Santorini episode.

Two eggs with puzzles solved.

Five more from Javier's collection. Helen

wondered if those six or seven had come from Palmeiro's vault or if a few of them had been tortured out of Ondrej's safekeeping.

And then there were those three duds via Santorini, containing their ticket to freedom —possibly.

Ten eggs altogether.

Whatever secrets they had held for seventy-seven years, they were about to spill soon.

According to Mom earlier, three of the eggs had been hers and Ondrej's—those she had known to exist.

It was spectacular that Mom had been able to unravel two puzzle eggs in such a short time period without the use of computers or guidebooks.

At first Helen had been surprised, but then she remembered what Palmeira had said. Mom's biological mother, Helena, had been a whizz at puzzles. She might have taught Mom something along the way.

Why had Javier picked Mom to do this dirty task?

What about others? There were many puzzle enthusiasts in the world. Why burden a sixty-eight-year-old grandma with the pain of an unsolvable Gordian knot?

"Lord Jesus, I pray for Mom. Heal her. And I

pray for Reuben. Keep him safe." The rest of her prayer was unspoken.

Let Leland and Dario track down Reuben.

Let Mom get a doctor.

Let us go home.

Burn down this place—after we leave!

Slowly, Helen began to sing a hymn until Mom dozed off.

Sitting against the wall, Helen was feeling sleepy herself. She had no idea the time of night, but it had to be way past three or four in the morning.

She could not hear any sound—no thunder or rain—so either this place was soundproof, or they were deep in the earth somewhere. The room was cool, but she didn't hear any air conditioner kick in, so a cave was a very likely scenario.

After Mom had fallen asleep, Helen gently placed her head on the carpet.

She returned to the table.

There were seven unopened eggs.

Could she unlock these puzzles? Crack these eggs?

"I have to tell you something, in case I don't make it out of here." Mom's voice was soft, but Helen could hear her clearly in the noiseless room.

"Mom, I thought you were asleep," Helen said. "Besides, you will get out of here. We will."

"We never know, do we?"

Helen blinked. "That's true. We never know how long we'll live. But God knows. He said the very hair of our heads are numbered."

Numbered.

She picked up one of the unopened Petros eggs. Shook it. It was very dense. If she could only twist it open. But no, the makers of these eggs had to create something complicated and frustrating.

She noticed that the egg could spin. And that it spun in a certain pattern. It reminded her of the puzzle structures that Dad had taught her to solve.

Funny how it went. Dad had taught Helen to solve puzzles, but he had taken Sabine to the gun range.

Helen stared at the egg. It was pretty with embedded precious stones. She didn't know what their names were, but there were at least several cut emeralds and diamonds trimming it.

She began to count in tempo as the egg spun on the table.

Nothing happened.

"Let me have another look at it," Mom said.

Helen plopped down on the floor next to Mom.

"Ah, that one. I couldn't figure it out." Mom

pointed. "I can't remember exactly, but this egg has almost the same design as the one that Fred gave to Agneta."

Agneta.

Helen was about to say something, when the door clicked open.

Javier came in with an entourage. He was dressed to go out, Helen noted.

"Not *almost*, Eleanora, but exactly the same egg." Javier motioned to his people.

Two of the men, including the guard whom Helen had met the night before—or whenever it had been—came forward and strong-armed Helen before she could push back.

Restrained, there was nothing a sleep-deprived Helen could do but watch with widened eyes as a woman prepared the syringe.

In a failed attempt to resist, Helen felt the needle in her neck.

Her world went dark.

CHAPTER EIGHTEEN

Helen awoke to the face of a young man staring down at her from a frame on the wall, his Renaissance eyes seemingly alive, as if saying, "You too?"

Helen blinked.

Raphael?

Having worked for ten years with the FBI Art Crime Team had its perks, and the ability to recognize a masterpiece was perhaps one of those.

Unless, of course, she was mistaken.

Fakes always abound.

She sat up, her tailbone sore from being plastered to the cold marble floor. She scooted toward the portrait. Gave herself a moment to regain her bearing in the less-than-ideally lit place, then stood up, palms flat against the wall for support as she inched toward the painting for a closer look.

There's no mistake.

"This can't be," Helen whispered to no one.

A cough behind her made Helen turned around.

"It is the *Portrait of a Young Man*," Mom said. "Such a shame that we may never be able to tell the world."

The oil painting by Raphael had been lost since World War II.

Helen sighed. Many works of art had disappeared in that war.

"How much do you think it's worth today?" Mom asked.

"More than the Petros eggs, I'm sure. But do we care?" Helen regretted her words as soon as she said it.

If this were a diversion for Mom, a moment of levity from their captivity, so be it.

Levity?

What am I talking about?

We are going to die!

"Check this out." Mom shuffled to a painting nearby, facing away from Helen.

Helen followed her.

"Humor me," Mom seemed to say in between the lines.

Mom spread out her hands and posed beside a framed painting of geometric patterns in light lemony yellow juxtaposed by white rectangles.

"I present to you the Le Pigeon aux petis pois." Mom smiled, her messy hair all askew on top of her head, her sleeves ripped in two or three places, scrapes up and down her arms, legs, and shoeless feet.

Helen's jaw dropped.

Pablo Picasso.

Her gaze traveled from Picasso's stolen painting back to Raphael's masterpiece, and then bounced all around the private collection of statues, urns, glass-cased jewelry pieces, and more paintings.

"What place is this?" Helen tried to remember how they had arrived here.

Her mind was one blindfold of nothingness.

She remembered the pinch of a syringe on her neck, blackness, and then waking up here.

That had been all.

"Where are we?" Helen asked.

"Why are we here? How long will we be here? What is the meaning of life?" Mom strutted toward an ornate table that looked like it had come from eighteenth-century France. "Any other important question, my daughter?"

It was a quiet room, save for their voices. Helen could not hear anything from outside the space they had been imprisoned. She wondered if they were underground again. If so, there was little hope of getting any GPS coordinates out to her rescue team.

Mom motioned for Helen to sit down on an equally antique chair adjacent to hers. "We have work to do."

"Is there?" Helen took her seat.

Lord Jesus, there has to be a way out of here —alive.

"While you were sleeping, Javier brought in the last two Petros eggs. Looks like Reuben has done it."

Reuben.

Helen wasn't sure if she wanted to hear that Reuben had returned to his old job. She remembered what she had said to him when they first met.

Once a thief, always a thief.

Could a thief change?

Could God change Reuben's heart?

Could he start to walk the straight and narrow path for the rest of his life, regardless of where he had come from?

CHAPTER NINETEEN

"Between the two of us, we have cracked all of two eggs," Mom said, almost too loudly.

Helen wondered if Mom expected Javier to be listening in. "You did all the work, Mom."

"We have a long way to go, but it's going to take time." Mom looked up at the ornate tray ceiling. "You got that, Javier?"

There you go.

It seemed surreal to Helen to be surrounded by stolen paintings, sculptures, and precious things their owners might never see again.

She stared at the nine eggs on the table. Mom had separated them into two groups.

Helen lifted one of the new eggs. "Mom?"

"Yeah?" And then Mom's coughing bouts began again. She coughed all over the egg in front of her, plus all over the table.

"Mom? You okay?"

"Just allergies. This room is dustier than the previous one."

Helen placed a hand on Mom's wrist. "Maybe we should rest a bit."

"No. You see that cuckoo clock over there?" Mom pointed to a German model on the wall. "We have ten hours to break these."

"Ten hours to break puzzles that had been hidden for seventy-seven years."

"Or he will cut off Reuben's fingers one by one."

"Seriously?" Helen remembered the touch of Reuben's fingers on her chin and neck that evening outside Palmeiro's ballroom.

They had put on a show, but it had felt real to Helen. Perhaps it had felt real to Reuben as well.

"According to Javier, Reuben could still hunt for eggs even if he were fingerless," Mom said.

No.

Helen couldn't imagine it. He had gone through so much, that Reuben. He had been born into a family of thieves, and it seemed that his choices had been few and far between.

Then again, when he had reached eighteen or twenty, couldn't he simply have walked away from a life of crime?

Ironically, his turning point had been in prison.

Sometimes we don't know what God lets us go through to clean us up and refine us.

"Get to work, Helen." Mom's voice turned sharp. "If not for me, then in the memory of your dad. We can't die in this vault."

Dad.

Helen remembered the pocket watch that she had given to Reuben. Had he activated it? Had he figured it out?

Were Leland and Dario on their way?

Helen knew she had to make sure. She put down one of the newly acquired eggs. "So which of these are the eggs that you brought to Oia?"

Mom pointed them out. "Why?"

Before Helen could answer her, Mom's lips curled into a smile. "You're your father's daughter, through and through. But..."

Helen knew what Mom wanted to say.

Uncle Javier had disabled the GPS receivers.

Otherwise, Helen and Mom would have been rescued by now.

"I'll still try," Helen said.

If she could reactivate the receivers...

Helen inspected the eggs, hoping to give an illusion that she was trying to solve more puzzles.

In a way, she was.

Extracting the Global Positioning System receivers inside the eggs with tools she didn't have would be near-impossible.

However, from her past history of working with INTERPOL, she could pretty much guess how they had inserted the GPS receivers into the eggs without first breaking the eggs.

According to Leland, the manual switch was a simple process.

It also meant that there was a high probability those eggs had been damaged somewhat. But if it worked out the way Helen thought it might, then she and Mom would be rescued.

Maybe.

God, help us.

Helen closed her eyes and prayed.

Tools. I need tools.

Her eyes darted here and there. This is a room full of paintings with frames and metal clasps, of jewelry with metal clasps...

Anything sharp and pointy around?

If she could get to the receivers, she could turn it on. How it had been turned off in the first place had been a mystery.

Could Mom have...?

She studied the three eggs from Mom's Santorini episode. Seemingly aware of what Helen was about to do, Mom looked like she was trying to keep a serious face and not be overly excited.

As soon as Javier found out that three of those Petros eggs were duds, both Helen and Mom would be dead.

Mom's life was worth more than all these eggs combined.

Much, much more.

"Tell me about Frederico and Agneta," Helen said, going to work.

CHAPTER TWENTY

"They were so in love." Mom sounded relieved to be able to get this secret off her chest all these years. "Frederico loved deeply."

Does his son love deeply too?

"Forty-four years ago, her parents disapproved. Fred was a poor fisherman's son from Spain, resettled in Italy, and moved around in Athens. A wanderer, you could say," Mom explained. "He didn't have the usual skills to get him a day job. But he could steal. And steal very well. He was the best thief I knew. Still, he couldn't stay put in one place."

"Hard to settle down if you move around all the time."

"Maybe. Maybe not." Mom shifted. She was clearly uncomfortable. "I met Agneta at a coffee shop at the university in Athens. I was an exchange student in graduate school at that time. She became my tour guide around town. We struck up a friendship."

Helen stared at the egg in her hand.

"She told me about this guy she had met who gave her jewelry. Agneta liked shiny things. But she was still living at home, and her parents had a bad feeling about Fred, who didn't seem to have a proper job."

"How old was he then?" Helen asked.

"In his late twenties, maybe? He could have been thirty years old. Something like that. I didn't ask."

"So he fell in love with a local girl."

"Originally, Agneta was from Thessaloniki, but their parents moved to Athens when she was a teen."

Helen waited for Mom to continue her story.

"Yes, they were infatuated with each other. Agneta was only twenty at that time. Though she had many boyfriends, she never brought them to her parents' house." Cough. Cough. "We worked out a scheme. Fred would come to my flat to see Agneta. I would go shopping for a couple of hours.

As things turned out, she got pregnant. She gave birth to a boy the next year."

Five years older than Reuben. "So Reuben has an older half brother, then."

"Can't be sure. We don't know if Fred was the father. Like I told you, she slept around." Mom shook her head. "But Fred was deeply in love, and to him, she could do no wrong."

"They never married?"

"This was before Fred met Reuben's mom, whom he also did not marry. I guess maybe he was waiting for Agneta to say yes. I don't know."

"Oh."

"Agneta didn't want to be a wife or mother."

"So... Who raised the child?"

"She gave him up for adoption." Mom sighed. "I finished university in Athens, met your dad, changed my career, and moved on. We loved being private investigators. It was a lot of fun for many years. But I wanted something more."

"Like skirting the law?" Helen frowned.

"Well, fifteen years ago, your dad and I were back in Athens. And some old friends called me."

"Frederico?"

Mom nodded. "He and Ondrej were still hunting for the lost Amber Room. Asked if I wanted to be a part of it. I knew that your dad would say it couldn't end well, but I was rebellious. I did it without his knowledge."

"How did you get out of the country?"

"I waited until your dad was away on a business trip."

Helen tried to recall that time when Dad had been alive. "Sabine and I must've been in college. I don't remember you and Dad traveling separately."

"We were always together. Except a couple of times. That was one of the times. The other one was when he flew to Toronto to see his sick grandmother. I was down with the flu and had to stay at home."

"And you gave Sabine the flu." The past should stay in the past. Too many memories to process.

Helen stared at the eggs.

"By then, Reuben was twenty-three years old," Mom said. "When I traveled with Fred to Thessaloniki to find Agneta, Reuben assumed I was the woman his father had fallen in love with. It worked into our narrative." Mom coughed again.

"How old was Agneta then?" Helen calculated that Mom had been in her early fifties when the friends reconnected.

"Fifty, poor, suffering, and married to an out-of-work loser. We all felt pity for her. Fred gave her a

Petros egg, not knowing she would try to sell it. Several days later, her husband was dead."

Helen waited for more.

"The catch was that Fred was there in the house when her husband was shot in the head."

"What was he doing there?"

"He was with Agneta in her bedroom, talking about Frederico supporting Agneta. Her husband walked in on them, and didn't like what he heard. Didn't want a handout. Whatever. A fight broke out. Somewhere in the middle of the fight a gun went off."

"Whose gun?"

Mom said she didn't know. "Fred was arrested for a murder to which he had confessed. Only I know this, but he said I wasn't to say a word."

"You kept your word."

"For fifteen years."

"So you let everybody think Frederico and you had something going—to take the focus off Agneta."

Mom nodded.

"What did Dad say about it?"

"He hated the idea."

"But you gave your word, though it was the wrong word."

Mom seemed to be deep in thought, as if debating whether to continue. "Three weeks after

Fred went to prison, Agneta walked in front of a bus. I spent the next several years visiting Fred in prison to continue the charade."

"But she was dead."

"Frederico insisted on keeping her memory pristine."

Helen had nothing to say to that.

"The egg?" she asked instead.

"It was never recovered."

"How many eggs did your little band of thieves steal?"

"Only three that I know of. That's what Ondrej kept for us. But Fred and Ondrej had been egg-hunting long before we met up again. They didn't tell me more than what I needed to know. I guess they were afraid I might have a change of heart and turn them in to the authorities."

"When will you tell Reuben the truth about you and his father?" Helen asked.

"Soon."

Helen was mulling over how to respond to Mom when she heard a spring snap on the egg that Mom had said Agneta tried to sell some fifteen years ago.

And just like that, the egg opened.

CHAPTER TWENTY-ONE

Out of the cracked egg rolled a piece of amber carved in the shape of an egg.

"Your dad has taught you well," Mom said.

"Yeah, all those years of working with puzzles... They are paying off now." Helen lifted the amber egg toward the light.

There was something inside.

Helen climbed on the chair and knelt down on the table to get the amber egg up close to the light-bulb above her. As she did so, the corner of her eye saw a colorful splash of light on her sweatshirt. She twisted the amber egg and turned it upside down and around until the light that shone through the amber egg projected something on the table.

A rectangular projection.

It looked like a photograph of a panel on a wall.

It was all reddish.

Amber-colored.

Helen hadn't had an opportunity to visit the Amber Room in the Catherine Palace. However, she had seen photos. Walls of amber, precious stones, and gold, carved by master craftspeople to reproduce what had been lost from the eighteenth century.

"The Petros eggs tell you where the Nazis had hidden some of the missing panels of the original Amber Room," Mom said. "Mind you, some of the hiding places have been bombed out by Allied Forces during World War II."

"Maps, are they?" Helen squinted. A magnifying glass would be needed to read any inscription on the eggs.

"Each panel is worth millions. More than each egg is worth."

"No wonder Javier wanted them."

Mom coughed. "Javier wants to recreate what his older brother had lost. He wanted an empire bigger than what Fred had started. Fred was a small-time jewel thief. Javier had grand ambitions."

Javier.

The name left a bad taste in Helen's mouth. And she didn't know the guy at all.

For now, to complete her plan, she needed Mom. "Let's solve as many of these puzzles as possible."

Mom tilted her head. "Why the sudden interest?"

"I want to go home," Helen said earnestly. "And Javier wants these eggs. I think we can work things out."

With a puzzled look on her face, Mom went to work.

Helen prayed that Javier would get them out of this vault with the eggs. Once out, the eggs should be able to send a clear signal to the GPS satellites.

"If we get just a few more done, maybe Javier will invite us to a meal so that we could show him the partial maps inside these eggs," Helen said. Loud enough, she hoped. "I'm sure he'd want to see all that have been hidden for seventy-seven years."

Javier hadn't taken the three solved puzzle eggs from them. He knew that all twelve eggs had to stay together.

And when he found out about the duds...

Helen prayed that they would not come to bloodshed.

As Helen and Mom had suspected, Javier had been listening to their conversation and had watched them work.

Some untold hours later, his guards ushered them out of the vault for this unexpected tea time with the enemy in a lavishly opulent sunroom.

Before tea, Mom showed Javier the three puzzles they had solved. Mom begged for more time.

"You were wrong, Eleanora," Javier said, when tea was served.

"About what?" Sitting on a rattan chair, Mom sipped her hot chai.

"About the number of people in Agneta's house that night." He looked relieved now that he had said it.

Mom didn't react. Neither did her cup and saucer shake.

Helen was quite impressed.

As for Helen, she couldn't bring herself to enjoy a cup of tea. She didn't want the memory of this moment to taint her future afternoons. Instead, she nibbled on a buttered scone. It had to make up for having missed several meals, at least.

Looking outside the sunroom, Helen was

surprised it was already afternoon. Another day had passed without her being aware of it. Or two days. Or more.

The day and night had all blended together in their windowless dungeon.

Helen prayed that Javier's cameras had not captured her activating the GPS receivers. She prayed that the signal was strong enough to reach INTERPOL.

The sunshine coming through the clear glass brightened the green fauna in the sunroom. Among ferns and greens were orchids of many varieties.

Where are we, exactly?

Dare I ask?

Helen let Mom do all the talking because the last thing she wanted was to make a scene. Her job as a PI probably wouldn't help the cause. Her favorite Glock had been confiscated by Javier's men back in Venice.

Her only weapons now were the three GPS receivers boosting one another in those eggs.

They were on the glass coffee table in front of her.

Come on, little eggs! You can do it!

Acting like smartwatches, all the three eggs had to do was find a satellite in space that spoke their language, lock onto it, and next thing they knew,

INTERPOL would pinpoint their location, wherever this place was.

All Helen and her mom had to do now was drink the tea, chat with Javier, and give the Global Positioning System time to pick up these eggs, and thus, their position.

And then Helen and Mom would go back to their hole in the ground to wait for a rescue.

"I don't think my brother would have told you everything," Javier added. "You're not family."

"Fred is dead." Slowly, Mom put down her cup and saucer on the coffee table. "Too little, too late to make amends."

"He was my big brother." Javier eyed the dozen Petros eggs on the table. "Frederico always protected me. And still does."

What does he mean by that? Helen couldn't read Javier's expressions. She waited.

"When I find all the panels, I will name the gallery Frederico's Amber Room."

"Such an impossible goal," Mom said. "Only fragments of the original room have been found in the last seventy years. Do you think you can do better?"

Javier lifted an egg and rotated it in the sunlight. "They don't have these keys."

Helen tried not to panic. She quickly prayed that the GPS receivers would not fail them.

Is it okay to pray over a piece of equipment?

God does care about the details of our lives, doesn't He?

"A number of people have died for those eggs," Mom said.

Javier shrugged. "Only Frederico, Ondrej, Agneta, and that good-for-nothing husband of hers."

"You have no family left."

"You're mistaken again." Javier sat back in his armchair. "I have family, the same family Frederico was trying to protect that night."

"What do you mean?" Helen finally asked.

"I was in Thessaloniki, yes, but I didn't go to Agneta's house. Not that night." Javier didn't look at either one of them. "Agneta and I—Frederico drove there himself."

"Who else did, then?" Mom asked. "Was Ondrej there?"

"I have no idea where Ondrej was." Javier straightened up. He motioned for his security detail to escort the ladies and the Petros eggs back to the cave. "Finish the rest."

On the way downstairs, it dawned on Helen what Javier had confessed to.

I didn't go to Agneta's house. Not that night...

Agneta and I...

"Agneta and you what, Javier?" Helen mumbled.

The guard must have heard her mutterings. He stopped. Then he continued walking. He opened the door of the vault to let them in.

As Helen passed by him, she tried to read his face. He was probably in his early forties, but had spent a lot of time in the sun. That was when she saw his eyes.

They were very light brown.

Like Javier Costa's.

CHAPTER TWENTY-TWO

After what seemed like hours, Helen didn't feel like working on the other eggs anymore. Whatever work they did would only go to Javier.

So far in what seemed like a long night, she had cracked another egg. Mom was working on one more.

That would add up to four out of twelve puzzles solved.

Three of the remaining puzzles could only be unraveled at INTERPOL.

That would leave five eggs to break.

Some host Javier had been. In the untold hours that Helen and Mom had been in the vault, they had been allowed to go to the bathroom once. Their only sustenance was a shared bottled water.

Bread? They had not been given food except for those scones Helen had eaten at tea time.

So why should they bother working anymore?

The invitation to tea had been a godsend. Helen prayed it was enough for the GPS satellites to pick up their location.

All they had to do now was to buy time, stretch the hours, until her SOS reached Leland and Dario. Even though the radio signals could be dampened again once they returned to their underground prison, at least it had been active for maybe an hour. That would have to be enough.

The rest was up to Leland, Dario, and INTERPOL.

Whether dead or alive, Helen and her mom would be found.

She prayed that Reuben would also be fine.

Reuben.

Helen's mind drifted to happy thoughts of being with him, from the time he had tackled her to the side of the lane in Santorini to their evening kiss in the storm...

"No matter what happens, I love you," Mom said to Helen.

"I love you too, Mom," Helen said.

"They took my pocket watch," Mom said.

"No, it's with the Athens police. It must've fallen out of your pocket."

Mom's eyes lit up. "Good. That's all I have left from your dad."

"We have one another too, Mom—you, Sabine, me—and we have God."

Mom shook her head. "You and Sabine have God. I have only myself."

"You can have God too, Mom. I will pray for you."

"I need all the prayer I can get."

"It's not the prayer itself, Mom. It's to Whom we pray. It makes a lot of difference whether you pray to a rock—or an egg—or to God."

Mom shook her head. "Those eggs have been my Achilles's heel for fifteen years. I'm glad it'll be over soon."

"Me too."

"When we get home to Savannah, I'm going back to church—oh, I may not go home to Savannah."

"We'll pray for favor with the judge. You've tried your best to make amends."

"Maybe they'll have church in prison. I'll attend."

"You talk about church in every crisis." Helen

chuckled. "Didn't you tell Sabine that you'll go to church, when you two were stuck in that trailer with the golden retriever?"

"I guess. I can't remember. I hope Sabine doesn't worry too much about us."

"She's stronger than us, Mom. I'm sure our church is also praying for our safety. Don't worry."

"That's what I'm supposed to tell you. Don't worry." Mom closed her eyes again. "I will finally have my rest. Do you know how tough it is to carry this burden in my chest? It's going to be lifted soon."

Helen fell asleep at the table, and dreamed of World War II bunkers and aircraft noises overhead. The bombings were loud and extremely close, as if the wall next to them was being blown out.

Helen awoke with a start.

And stared straight into the muzzle of a Heckler & Koch MP5 submachine gun.

"Time to go home, ladies."

Italian words never sounded so sweet.

CHAPTER TWENTY-THREE

Reuben climbed out of an SUV outside Uncle Javier's Villa Isidora, at the edge of the little town of Tremezzo on Lake Como. A soft breeze from the calm lake greeted him, welcoming him to the scenic towns of Lombardy.

Ah, to come here under more felicitous circumstances...

Four days ago, Reuben had no idea that his uncle had owned this villa, let alone imprisoned Helen Hu and her mother in it.

Still, a lot had happened in four days.

As soon as Dario had tracked down Helen's pocket watch to Reuben and beaten off his handlers, the case had been turned over to

INTERPOL Venice. The local police then surrounded Uncle Javier's villa in that old city, raising Reuben's hope to see Helen again.

Unfortunately, it had been a false positive. They found the villa completely deserted.

Since then, Reuben had prayed endlessly for God's deliverance.

His hopes had gone up again when Dario reported that they had detected faint radio signals coming from some handheld GPS unit that had used the same frequencies of the three eggs that Mama Hu had delivered to her contacts in Santorini not too long ago.

Dario, Leland, and CIA analysts had tracked the signal all over Italy. As soon as they had pinpointed the point of origin of those beacons, the entire country's law enforcement officers descended on the picturesque Lake Como.

The *polizia provinciale* and the *polizia di stato* had worked hard all night long to coordinate this raid. Reuben had nothing but praise for the provincial and the state police officers working together with a team from Italy's Arma dei Carabinieri armed forces to disable Uncle Javier's security detail.

Still.

Reuben felt alone, and yet he wasn't. He was

standing with the police, and not against them. That had been his comfort.

That, and the fact that God was with him.

In what seemed like ages, Reuben finally saw Uncle Javier being escorted out of Villa Isidora in his silk pajamas and steel handcuffs. Several of his security forces had cuts and bruises on them. One even came out on a cot.

Eventually, Reuben spotted Helen and Mama Hu walking out on their own volition. Mama Hu climbed onto a cot as she reached closer to the curved driveway.

Reuben's heart skipped a beat as he quickened his pace. He felt relieved.

It's finally over.

Coming out of the villa behind the hostages, for all the world to see, were the Petros eggs, five of them in a special case, carried proudly by an investigator from the Comando Carabinieri per la Tutela del Patrimonio Culturale, Italian's cultural police that chased after art thieves like Uncle Javier, and who had been keeping a watchful eye on the aging Palmeiro.

Reuben wondered if Helen would give him the time of day as soon as she found out he really had stolen two more Petros eggs for Uncle Javier, regardless of whether he had done it to gain his uncle's trust.

Perhaps she had already known about it. He wished he had time to put a message in the last two eggs.

If the twelve eggs were supposed to be the key to unlock a vault of something, time would tell if they would yield dividends in the future.

For now, their secrets remained locked.

It was the turn of museum experts to crack the eggs, follow the trails, figure it all out.

Reuben was done. Tired.

Helen was at the back of the ambulance, receiving treatment. She looked okay from this distance. They would all go to the hospital for evaluation.

And then home.

Reuben waved to Mama Hu. She smiled wryly. Then coughed a lot.

Helen looked his way. "May I have my pocket watch back?"

Reuben placed the pocket watch in Helen's palm, then pulled her to his chest.

She wrapped her arms around his waist, and rested her head on his shoulder.

He knew then that she had missed him too.

INTERPOL agent Damiano Kolovos reached

the ambulance shortly after Reuben had. "Well done."

"You now have to crack the rest of the eggs to have the key to whatever it is," Reuben said.

"Well, no. They're under Italian jurisdiction now with the help of the Russian Consulate," Kolovos explained. "The Carabinieri force has contacted the Russian Consulate, and we'll let the archaeologist and cryptanalysts work it out."

"You?" Reuben had always been naturally curious. Kolovos was a good man, and Reuben hoped to keep in touch.

"Since I've passed the baton on to INTERPOL Rome, I shall return to Athens for a bit of rest and holiday, and then it's on to my next case," Kolovos said.

"Will they invite us to the dig, if they find out where the Amber Room panels are?" Helen asked.

"I'll see what we can do. For now, go rest and take it easy." Kolovos eyed Mama Hu's cot. "We're going to fly your mother back to Athens. She still has a court date."

Helen nodded. "I'll be there."

"And to be sure, since she has helped the authorities, the court will take that into consideration."

Reuben nodded at Kolovos's encouraging

words. Perhaps Mama Hu wouldn't be in prison until the day she died.

Before Reuben realized it, Helen had gone to be by Mama Hu's side.

"Take care of your sister," Mama Hu said. "And your dad's legacy. He'll be so proud of you, as I am."

"I'm coming to see you in Athens as soon as they let me," Helen said. "Don't worry."

"I'm not worried, really. I'm rather relieved."

"I bet." Reuben came up beside Helen. "I'm in Athens too, and I'll go see you."

"You better," Mama Hu said. "We have much to talk about your dad."

"I'm sorry I thought it was you who broke his heart."

"Many women broke your dad's heart, but I wasn't one of them." Mama Hu shrugged. "Let's talk about something happier. Your dad would be glad to see how well you've turned out."

Reuben could hardly get the words out. He just nodded.

CHAPTER TWENTY-FOUR

O n a warm Santorini afternoon two months later, Helen Hu found Reuben Costa sitting on a lounge chair on his rooftop patio and talking to a cat on his lap.

She stood there at the bright-blue gate, leaning against it, really, for strength.

The cat looked her way.

So did Reuben.

He stared.

"You have a cat," Helen said.

"Adopted him from the no-kill shelter. Meet Petros."

"Petros. Nice name. Keeps you company?"

"While I waited for you." A smile followed his words. "I wasn't sure if you'd come back."

"I wasn't sure either." Helen looked out to the sea and sky, toward the same mountains, the same deep ocean, the depth of which she could not fathom.

Just like their relationship.

"I had to see you," Helen said. "But you knew that."

"Yes. Emails, messages, texts, phone calls, Face-Time, and so forth aren't enough, are they?"

"No." Helen watched Reuben let the cat go.

Then Reuben left the lounge chair and walked toward Helen. He had on a pair of flip-flops. His loose-fit pair of blue linen pants flapped in the sudden burst of wind. His white shirt, buttoned to his collarbone, also flitted about, the rolled-up sleeves revealing a deeper tan than before.

Freedom had its benefits. Time in the sun and all that.

When he reached Helen, so did that familiar, clean smell of fresh soap and his eau de cologne.

Reuben held her hand. His hand was warm, like the afternoon sun, like a cup of chai, like...

Love?

Somewhere in the catacombs of their adventures together in Greece and Italy, perhaps Helen had fallen in love.

"Have you?" Reuben ran a thumb along Helen's jaw.

"Have I what?"

"Have you fallen in love?"

Helen froze. "I wasn't thinking aloud."

"No, but I saw it in your eyes." Reuben stepped closer until their shoulders touched. "You remember our kiss."

Well, that hadn't been what Helen was thinking, but now that he had mentioned it, she did remember the kiss.

In the rain. In the lightning and thunder.

In the storm.

"We've been through a lot together," Reuben added.

Helen nodded.

"Would you like to sit down?" Reuben asked. "Have something to drink? Mineral water? Soda?"

"There's only one chair." Helen pointed to the lounge chair.

"I'll get a chair from the kitchen. Or you can sit on my lap."

What a tease.

"Not on cat hair." Helen pointed to his blue pants.

"I don't see any."

Helen heard something in the air, and turned toward the noise. It was a drone. Taking photos of the village of Oia and the surrounding landscape.

Probably harmless.

Still, she felt a sudden urge to duck. To run downstairs. To hide.

Reuben must've sensed it.

He reached for her hand again. "Let's go inside."

Helen didn't move. "I'm all right. It's probably taking videos of the sunset."

Reuben glanced at his watch. "In less than an hour."

"I guess I came at the right time."

"How about dinner with me tonight?" Reuben asked. There was hesitation in his voice.

"Sure," Helen said. If that had assured him somewhat, she couldn't tell.

Reuben's rental house was at the top of the pile of boxy houses. To their right were a couple of blue church domes. Below this hilltop patio were more cliff-hugging buildings.

Among the buildings, tourists poured down the steps and narrow lanes, looking for balconies to park themselves and set up video cameras and smartphones for their sunset viewing.

The noise of people and drones and distant airplanes sort of destroyed any peace and quiet on this volcanic rock of an island.

Helen leaned against Reuben's shoulder. "Will they let you come to the States?"

Why am I asking him that?

Surely the INTERPOL needs his expertise.

"Only to see you. I'm a free man now, though I only work behind the scenes."

Helen wondered about that.

"I know you had to do some work stateside for two months, and I waited for you," Reuben added. "I wanted to fly to Savannah to see you, but you were incommunicado."

Helen couldn't tell him more—not at this time. Her undercover work required secrecy. This was the first time she had a chance to fly to Santorini to see Reuben again since July. To contact him sooner would have endangered her mission and her team.

"How is your uncle doing?" Helen asked.

"Uncle Javier?"

"Is there another?"

Reuben laughed. "So far he's the only uncle I know, but more relatives could come out of the woodwork later. Let's hope not all of them are in prison."

"Your uncle probably hadn't expected to be

caught, tried, and put into prison." Ironically, catching Javier had helped reduce Mom's sentence.

"He writes me from time to time from Rome. Prison cells and his lifestyle don't go too well together—if I read his handwritten letters correctly."

Some seabirds squawked above them.

"Since I was in prison for years, I offered some advice for him regarding how to survive it," Reuben continued.

Helen didn't know what to say about prison life and was grateful to be distracted by a meow.

The cat returned.

"Hello, Petros." Helen picked him up. He purred.

Reuben nodded. "He likes you."

And then the cat leapt off Helen's arms.

"I went to see Mom yesterday," Helen said after watching the cat disappear down some steps. "Gave her a large-print Bible."

"Good. How is she?"

"Doing the best she can, given the circumstances. Her biggest concern is not being able to get her nails done, but she's teaching the other fellow prisoners Mandarin Chinese, and they're helping her remember how to speak Greek, so it's working out."

The visit to the Athens women's prison had been too brief, but it was better than nothing. Helen wondered how she could see Mom more often. She had originally intended for Hugo to run the European branch of her private investigation firm, but now...

Now Helen would like to move here herself, if it meant she could be closer to Reuben.

Hugo could go back to Savannah and manage the main office there.

"Mom says you've been to see her several times in the last two months." Helen's voice caught. "You're too kind."

"You were busy, and she was lonely."

"You did it for me."

Reuben rested his arm over Helen's shoulders. "For you, yes."

"God's mercy cleans up a lot of messes in our families, doesn't it?"

"Only God." Reuben squeezed her shoulder.

Helen sniffled.

"Cheer up. Your mom's fine. Like she said, she's relieved to finally pay for what she had done. Besides, she likes to talk about you, so..."

"Me? What does she say about me?" Trying not to be alarmed, Helen was curious.

"She is betting you'll say no when I propose to you."

"Why would I say no?" Helen blurted.

"You would say yes?"

Silence.

"Wait here." Reuben left her standing on his roof.

CHAPTER TWENTY-FIVE

Helen heard a few doors open. Reuben must have left them ajar, because the next time she heard the doors shut, it was only moments before he returned to the flat-roof patio.

In Reuben's open palm was a jewel-encrusted egg. It shone pink and purple and blue in the Santorini sun. If there was anything Helen knew about the Costa family...

Helen's eyes widened.

He chuckled. "Don't worry. It's a replica."

Helen's hands clutched against her chest. "It'd better be."

"But what's inside is one of a kind."

"What is it?"

"Open it and see."

Helen wanted to guess first, but she also wanted to know right away. More secrets? Or something as benign as a pendant? A bracelet? A brooch?

Slowly, she opened the bejeweled pyxidium.

And gasped.

On a plush velvet bed was a ruby ring. So red—like a flaming fire in the late afternoon sun—the ruby was surrounded by a ring of diamonds that now sparkled.

Helen blinked.

She was about to say something, when she noticed that Reuben was on his knees.

What in the world?

He was grinning like a schoolboy.

They stared at each other for the longest time.

"Something you want to say?" Helen finally asked.

"Something to ask." Reuben didn't break their eye contact.

Helen closed her eyes.

"Look at me, love." Reuben reached for Helen's elbows. She still held the egg.

Helen's eyelids fluttered open.

"I love you, Helen Hu. Marry me."

I want to say yes, but... "Where will we live? Savannah? Santorini?"

"Home is wherever God leads us, sends us, puts us," Reuben said. "You asked me earlier if I could travel to the US. I told you *yes*."

Helen nodded.

"I've prayed about this for the last two months that we've been apart. I know I've got a past that's not stellar, but I paid my dues—"

Helen had to cut him off. "It's not that."

This time last year, Helen would have written him off as someone she could never date. However, Reuben had finished his prison sentence and was now a free man.

His soul was even freer since the day he had accepted Jesus Christ as his personal Lord and Savior.

In prison, no less.

Ironically, Helen's own mom was now incarcerated. She would be well into her eighties when they let her out of prison.

Helen's lips quivered.

"Not my criminal record?" Reuben asked.

"That's in the past." Helen swallowed. "Yes, there were sowing and reaping, but the guilt of your sins has been paid for at the cross of Christ. You still have to go through the consequences of your thieving days, but your soul is now blameless in Christ."

"That's a sermon." Reuben chuckled. "Should I get a cushion so my knees are not on this hard floor while I listen to you?"

"Oh, stand up then."

"Not until you answer my question." Reuben took the egg from Helen and reached for her left hand with his free hand. "Will you marry me, Helen Hu?"

"Yes."

Helen's hands trembled as she watched Reuben slide the tight cluster of ruby and diamonds onto her ring finger. "Since that night..."

Reuben's eyes met hers. "On the veranda in Venice?"

"Yes, just before we were abducted."

They laughed.

"Since that night, that kiss, I knew we had something serious going," Helen said.

"I shall have to kiss you like that the rest of my life then," Reuben said.

"I expect nothing less. Do start right away."

"Yes, love." And he didn't disappoint.

CHAPTER TWENTY-SIX

It had taken over a hundred historians, archaeologists, cryptographers, and amateurs working together to solve the puzzle eggs that had been found and to find their connection to the Amber Room.

Helen was pleased that the Athens court had reduced Mom's years in prison due to her continual cooperation with INTERPOL, the FBI, and the Russian government to recover panels of the Amber Room.

Already two fragments had been discovered in underground tombs in Vienna and Berlin.

Now the search had reached the happy city of Heraklion, Crete, to a lonely crypt at the back of an old, crumbling church.

Agneta Sanna's crypt.

Helen stood at the edge of the excavation site, taking videos of the scene. Next to her, Reuben was doing the same. Snap. Snap.

She wondered about the secrets that had been buried with Agneta for fifteen years. Today, they would peek into what was beneath.

The Petros eggs that Helen and her mom had worked on in Javier's Villa Isidora had put INTER-POL, the FBI Art Crime Team, and various departments of antiquities from Italy all the way to Russia on a nine-month quest to find at least one wall of amber, stolen from Russian history.

No one had thought of checking Agneta's burial ground in Crete, of all places.

Why Crete? That was an answer that Frederico Costa had taken with him to the grave.

The first excavation had begun around and inside the crypt days ago.

When Helen glanced over to see how Reuben was reacting to the possible find, she spotted someone in the crowd.

At first she thought it was a younger version of Javier. Maybe in his forties.

But on a second look, Helen realized it was one of Javier's guards, who looked like his employer—now serving the rest of his life in a Roman prison.

That guard must've escaped somehow and evaded the roundup at Javier's Villa Isidora.

Helen tugged at Reuben. He tilted his ear toward her.

"Behind you," she whispered. "Looks like one of the guards in Javier's villa in Tremezzo."

"I don't see anyone," Reuben whispered back.

"I'm going to text Kolovos."

"I thought they're all in jail."

"Maybe he got out. Or he never went in."

In any case, he was Kolovos's problem now, not theirs anymore.

Someone came out of the crypt to make an announcement that they had found something, throwing the crowd into a cheering frenzy and putting the Hellenic Police force on full alert all around the crypt and graveyard.

Helen clapped along with everyone else in attendance.

"It could be days before we have the next piece of information, so please be patient," the representative said.

Nearby, reporters resumed broadcasting in various languages. Within earshot of Helen, a BBC reporter was interviewing a professor of antiquities from Athens.

"If they do find even one panel of the Amber

Room, it would probably be very fragile and in poor condition," she said.

"Well, we know that the Russian curators of the Catherine Palace outside St. Petersburg would be thrilled to death—no pun intended—if we find anything amber today," the reporter said. "Thank you for being with us, Professor Antonis."

The reporter concluded by saying that this find would lead to other excavations around Europe.

Helen knew that the same process would be repeated at various sites up and down Europe, tracing the paths of a war-torn past in the hope of finding trails and maps to lost panels of the Amber Room.

Still, they might not find what they sought. The Amber Room, glorious as it might have been, could have been lost to history and World War II. Only God knew where those amber walls had been hidden. Treasure hunters had searched for decades, to no avail. Why would their counterparts today fare any better?

For Helen and Reuben, this was as far as they would go.

It was time to move on from a long and difficult past.

Palmeiro had been declared too old to be sent

to prison, and he had given up all his fortunes and stolen goods to the state to be returned to their rightful owners.

As life sometimes was, Palmeiro was diagnosed with brain cancer only a couple of weeks ago, and that would be his short and suffering prison.

Helen and Reuben had promised to take some videos of this historic event so that Palmeiro could see that he had been a part of history.

Helen could not get used to calling him Grandfather, and she had not even tried. Some day she might.

As for Mom, sitting in prison, she was all too happy to find out her own father was still alive. Though they could not see each other, they could talk on the phone.

And that had to be enough for both of them.

"Ready to go?" Reuben asked. "I'm running out of battery on my dinky smartphone. And there will probably be no news until later, anyway."

Helen was glad that Reuben decided to use a smartphone again. As with all things, there was a learning curve, but at least he could text her.

"I know we have a wedding to finish planning, but I feel like taking the rest of the day off, since it's a Saturday and all." Helen sighed.

"We'll keep the wedding simple." Reuben put an arm around her waist. "We've decided on a laid-back honeymoon in Oia, where we met. What could possibly go wrong?"

Helen didn't respond.

A lot was on her mind. Wedding planning... Work. Mostly work.

Work was quite heavy for her these days. Moving an office from Brussels to Athens had been a chore, if not for the helpful assistance of Reuben, who spoke fluent Greek.

Helen had already decided to offer him the job of office manager and local liaison.

As for her Savannah office, she had been talking to her sister and brother-in-law about their running the office there. Ming Wei had his own PI firm, but they had been discussing merging them for years. Perhaps it would finally happen.

If it didn't happen, Hugo would continue to manage her Savannah office.

More things to add to the prayer list.

"Time for lunch?" Reuben asked.

"Is it already? Let's go then. We can follow this excavation online." On the way to their car, Helen spotted Kolovos and a local police officer talking to Javier's guard.

Quietly, he let them handcuff him. Before they took him away, he glanced in Helen's direction.

She patted Reuben's arm. "See?"

Reuben turned.

And froze.

CHAPTER TWENTY-SEVEN

The anonymous phone call an hour before her wedding processional caught Helen by surprise. It came at a very bad time. Fortunately for the caller, Helen had her phone in hand as her sister helped her put on her wedding gown.

"Helen, please." Sabine fussed with the long vertical row of buttons on Helen's back. "Don't answer the call."

"I have to. It's work."

"This is your day off."

"When do I ever get a day off?"

"Christmas, Thanksgiving, Easter, and on your wedding day, sis." Sabine stepped around the white laces on Helen's gown. "Sit down and I'll put on your shoes for you."

"Hold on a sec." Helen's mind was elsewhere, far away from the stateroom she is in. She walked toward the porthole overlooking the Mediterranean. The yacht was away from shore, but...

Something bothered her.

The fact that the caller knew her personal number made her more than antsy. She called Hugo McCall in Brussels to verify the call and trace the source.

"How much time do we have until the wedding?" Helen asked Sabine after she hung up the phone.

"An hour and fifteen minutes."

"Good." Helen speed-dialed Leland Yang-Joule, as the door opened and the wedding photographer came in.

Amy Untermeyer-Theroux was seven months along, but she wore a coat over her baby bump. She held one camera in her hand. Behind her, an assistant carried two cameras around his neck and a backpack.

"I need five minutes, uninterrupted," Helen said to Sabine.

Sabine nodded, sighing. She knew her sister

well. She ushered Amy and her assistant out of the stateroom, and closed the door behind her.

Leland picked up after several rings. Her voice sounded groggy. It was morning in Atlanta—nearly sunset in Santorini—but Leland worked around the clock and slept whenever she could.

Helen explained what was going on, and Leland sprung into action.

With the hacker's help, Helen and Hugo tracked down the call to a cell phone in a cafe in Cannes. When their local contacts reached it, they found the cell phone in a dumpster behind the cafe, with photographs of a middle-aged woman in sunglasses sipping cappuccino at a restaurant table.

The woman's name was Philomena Caddock.

And sure enough, there were fishing vessels out at sea. Nothing unusual about that.

Sabine held the satin sandals in her hand, waiting to put them on her sister's feet, when the second call came.

"Please," the woman said. "Jake Kessler is in the *Le Crevette Rose*. Molyneux will kill him if you don't get there in time."

Molyneux?

FBI Special Agent Jake Kessler? The one who had gone deep undercover in Molyneux's organization?

Remain calm. Remain calm. "Tell me who you are."

"I'm sorry." The line disconnected.

She sounded like the same caller. This time, there was more urgency, and she gave more information, like the name of the fishing vessel.

Helen called Leland and Hugo. "Did you get that?"

"Yes," Leland said.

"A stroke of genius to let us tap your phone," Hugo said.

"After this, I'm getting a new phone and new number." Helen chuckled.

"She is easy to trace because she wants to be traced," Leland added.

"Yes, because she wants me to trust her. She doesn't want to be known, but she wants us to know she has credible information."

Nearby, Sabine pointed to her watch. It was time.

Helen nodded to her, but she was still on the phone. "Hugo, what's the fastest way to get a chopper to this yacht? You know where I am."

"Dario de la Cruz is somewhere in Europe today, I think. Wonder if he's available?"

"He will be once you tell him what's going on. However, *somewhere* is the problem. We don't know where he is, and there's no way to contact him." In fact, Helen had invited the CIA agent to her wedding, but he did not want to show his face in public, even though the wedding was at sea. He preferred to remain under the radar, hunting for terrorists at large, such as the elusive Molyneux. "How about INTERPOL?"

"Damiano Kolovos is in Athens, finishing up paperwork on Molyneux."

"Good. We'll give him more to write about. Call him."

"Will do, ma'am."

"And don't forget the chopper. I need it ASAP." Helen ended the call, wishing that Hugo wasn't such a workaholic. She had invited every employee at Hu Knows, Inc., to her wedding, but someone had to stay behind at their European branch office in Brussels.

Speaking of wedding, she was running late.

Easing on the side of caution, Helen rejected her wedding shoes and stepped into her favorite boots, all the while wondering how to explain to her husband-to-be what they had to do.

Well, that could be a test for him.

CHAPTER TWENTY-EIGHT

ama Hu didn't want them to delay the wedding until she was out of Korydallos Prison. By the time of her release, she would be well into her seventies. Both Helen and Reuben would be in their late forties.

All things considered, having Mama Hu alive was more than Reuben could have asked. It had been one of the best gifts God had given to them, and he couldn't complain.

As he waited for his bride to get ready in her stateroom, Reuben prayed again. He had prayed so many times that he had lost count. Prayed for his own nerves, for Helen's nerves, for Mama Hu not to be too sad that she couldn't attend the wedding. They'd send her a video of the event later.

Pacing the polished deck of the private yacht, Reuben prayed one more time, for good measure.

He even prayed for Uncle Javier and his long-lost cousin, Nikos Ioannidis, both serving time in Rome.

It turned out that those two men had known each other for the last fifteen years. After Father had gone to prison, Uncle Javier somehow met up with Nikos, whom he had thought was Father's illegitimate son with Agneta.

Nikos had thought the same. After he had become an adult, he traveled back to Thessaloniki to find his mother. Agneta had welcomed him, but her then-husband hated Nikos. When Agneta's husband and Frederico got into an argument, Nikos had snapped and shot his mother's husband in the head.

Frederico had taken the blame, pushing him out the back door into the night. Sadly, while he had been in prison, he still tried to protect Nikos, whom he had thought was his firstborn son.

In the end, Father had died without knowing the truth.

The truth had only been revealed days before Agneta died in the traffic accident. Poverty and Agneta hadn't gotten along well, and when Frederico gave Agneta a Petros egg, she assumed that the entire Costa family was rich.

When Frederico had gone to prison for a crime he did not commit, the only person Agneta could go to for money was Javier.

And she had a leverage. Nikos was Javier's heir.

Ah. Each family had its own problems.

Reuben was glad God had led him out of the dark crime pit. He had a decent job with INTER-POL. Yes, the pay was much less than what he had earned back in the bad old days, but the compensation of freedom was too priceless to give up.

The Lord had been good to Helen as well. Her Athens office was running smoothly. She had hired additional private investigators.

They had bought that tiny house in Santorini, where Reuben had proposed to her, and turned it into their vacation home.

The little house on top of the village of Oia would be where they'd spend their wedding night. Next week they would fly home to Athens, where they had been scoping out some city dwellings. Helen kept her house in Savannah, Georgia, where they would spend half the year.

Someone sat down next to him.

Helen's pastor from Riverside Chapel in Savannah, Pastor Diego Flores was perhaps five or six years older than Reuben. Flores and Reuben had struck up a budding friendship. It had turned out that Flores's mother was Italian, and his parents often visited family on the Amalfi Coast.

"Nice yacht," Pastor Flores said.

"Helen's reward for her hard work." Reuben didn't want to tell Pastor Flores more. The Russian Consulate in Athens had paid for the entire wedding, yacht and all.

"I wonder how much a one-day cruise like this costs, you know?" Pastor Flores asked.

"Beyond my budget, I'm sure." Once upon a time, Reuben's dad had sailed around the Mediterranean like this—with other people's money.

"Small change compared to what they got back," Pastor Flores said.

"Then again, the money would be better off spent on feeding the poor, yes?" Reuben added.

"True."

In no time, the wedding ceremony started as the sun began to set on Santorini that Friday evening in May, eight months after Reuben had proposed to Helen.

Reuben stood there grinning next to Pastor Flores, his eyes automatically sweeping across the faces in attendance. Only immediate family and close family friends were invited. Helen's only sister, Sabine, and her husband, Aidan Ming Wei, sat close to the front. Helen's two faithful employees, Hugo and Earl, were somewhere on the yacht.

For some reason, Helen had decided that they needed a security detail.

FBI Special Agent Camden La Salle, his lovely wife, Iris, and their bevy of well-behaved children, smiled at him. The children waved. They had been all over Reuben's cat, frightening him to bits. Petros had been hiding in closets and cupboards for days.

As the harp and violin transitioned into *Canon in D*, Reuben turned his head toward the two instrumentalists.

Ivan McMillan, Helen's musician friend from St. Simon's Island, was playing a Stradivarius. Reuben had been assured that it wasn't the 1698 Damaris Brooks that Helen and company had recovered for Ivan's wife, Brinley.

Next to the violinist, Emmeline O'Hanlon-Langston was playing a full-size concert harp. The talented harpist was forever grateful that Helen had helped her find her long-lost brother.

Truly, Reuben was proud of his wife-to-be.

Speaking of Helen, where in the world was she?

The sun was going to set soon. Didn't she know?

The music transitioned again, and there came the bride, beaming under her veil.

Reuben chided himself for his own impatience. He decided to apologize to Helen later.

That was, until he saw Helen's boots.

Underneath the white lace and beads and silk and tulle, Helen was wearing laced-up black boots.

Oh no.

Helen smiled broadly, sweetly.

Then Reuben spotted her ankle. Something was strapped there.

He opened his mouth to speak.

Helen locked her arms in his.

He forgot what he was about to say.

But something was up. Reuben could see it, smell it, feel it in the Aegean air.

Pastor Flores called everyone to attention, but Reuben lost his focus. He was there, yes, but his mind roiled around, asking God to calm him as he grew more and more concerned by the minute.

Her concealed firearm.

Her combat boots.

What else, Helen? What else?

Reuben caught Pastor Flores's glare.

Trying to keep his mind within the confines of the present ceremony, Reuben willed away his fears. A quick prayer brought him back to what mattered.

Pastor Flores read I Corinthians 13 in its entirety.

"You may kiss the bride." Pastor Flores nodded to Reuben.

Reuben couldn't remember who kissed whom first, but he thought that Helen seemed to be in a hurry. The flashes of a nearby camera made Reuben blink.

The sun was setting in the distant horizon, beyond the mountains cropping out of the ocean.

The noise of camera shutters made Reuben smile as happily as he could.

The very pregnant photographer probably hadn't missed the moment. Amy Untermeyer-Thoreux specialized in destination weddings, though she also owned a studio on River Street, back in Helen's hometown of Savannah.

Before they walked down the aisle to cheering family and friends, Reuben heard them.

Unmistakable, noisy blades thwacking closer and closer to his ears.

Everyone turned toward the noise.

It was then that Reuben realized the yacht had come to a standstill on the ocean as the helicopter hovered above it. It landed on the helipad on the top deck.

"Is that a late guest?" Reuben asked.

"That's our ride," Helen said.

"I thought we were going to honeymoon here in Santorini."

"Our wedding surprise."

"Don't you think we should've discussed this?"

"It wouldn't be a surprise then." Helen locked her fingers in Reuben's and pulled him along as she climbed the steps toward the helipad.

Reuben turned to everyone. "Thank you, everyone, for coming!"

They ran toward the chopper. When Reuben climbed in, someone in a helmet handed him his headset.

"Congratulations," he said.

Reuben recognized that voice.

Damiano Kolovos.

INTERPOL.

This is not a honeymoon!

Reuben glared at Helen. He spoke into his headset. "What kind of little adventure is this?"

"Don't you want to know who sent the armed drone to Oia last year when we first met?" Helen shut the chopper door.

"No," Reuben replied.

"What about how Javier and Nikos had funneled millions of euros to fund terrorist activities across Europe?"

"That's not our problem, is it?"

Helen ignored him. "You speak French, don't you?"

"Oh no. No, Helen. No, no, no."

"Yes, yes." Helen buckled her safety belt. She waved to the pilot to take off. "We only have a small window. Two days, maybe three at most."

"To do what?"

"To stop your family fortune from being used to purchase armed drones."

"Stop it."

"You know who's buying more drones?"

"I don't care, Helen. Don't bargain with me. Tell me the truth. Why are we in an INTERPOL chopper instead of at our wedding reception?"

Straight talk is always the best. Helen sighed. "We are needed in Cannes."

"Why?"

"Molyneux has taken a hostage out at sea."

"Moly—oh no, Helen. No. She's dangerous. Let someone else deal with her."

Helen must not have been listening. "After that, she's gone to who knows where, you know?"

"But it's our honeymoon," Reuben tried again.

"We can honeymoon in Cannes." Helen checked her magazine and Glock. "You'll like Cannes."

"Not while chasing down a terrorist."

"Well..."

"This is Molyneux we're talking about. She's the worst. She's a ruthless killer."

"Yep. Everybody wants her, from the CIA to MI6, from the FBI to INTERPOL. Now we join the hunt."

"Helen."

"They've been after her for several years. She's so elusive!"

"Helen."

"If we can get her first..."

"Helen."

"She's behind the armed drone. You remember the armed drone?"

"Helen!" His voice was stern now. Loud.

Too stern?

Apparently it didn't bother his new wife.

Helen leaned toward Reuben as far as her seat belt would extend. "We're just married. Let's not quarrel right away."

Reuben was too flabbergasted to respond.

Helen pushed away her mouthpiece, then his.

170

She wrapped her fingers around his neck, and pulled him gently toward her.

Her lips reached his chin. Then his cheek.

Her lips were warm, almost hot, by the time they reached his own lips.

The noise of the chopper blades above them faded away.

All Reuben could see and think of was his bride.

Reuben knew, then and there, that he would never let his wife out of his sight.

My wife. My very own wife.

Helen Costa.

Helen Hu-Costa.

Whatever she wants to call herself.

He would go with her wherever she wanted to go, even to the ends of the earth, and do whatever she wanted to do...

Even going after a dangerous fugitive on their honeymoon.

And there was no turning back.

Dear Reader:

I hope you enjoyed the action-adventure story of Helen and Reuben. *Once a Thief* hints at the discovery of panels from the lost Amber Room. That storyline continues in *Once a Hero*, in which our honeymooning couple makes a cameo appearance.

FBI Special Agent Jake Kessler takes the lead in *Once a Hero*, alongside treasure hunter Beatrice Glynn, who debuts in this second book in the Protector Sweethearts series. Both are looking for the Amber Room, which they hope will lead to Molyneux, the villain mentioned in *Reach for Me* (Vacation Sweethearts Book 2). In *Once a Hero*, we will finally see the denouement of this Molyneux subplot as well as the conclusion of the Amber Room mystery.

Once a Hero (Protector Sweethearts Book 2)
JanThompson.com/hero

Helen Hu's Previous Appearances

The events in *Once a Thief* happen after these stories, where Helen Hu makes several appearances. In fact, *Tell You Soon* is where we first meet Mama Hu.

- Tell You Soon (Savannah Sweethearts Book 2)
- Love You Always (Savannah Sweethearts Book 6)
- Reach for Me (Vacation Sweethearts Book 2)
- His Longing Heart (Seaside Chapel Book 1)
- His Wake-Up Call (Seaside Chapel Book 2)

In *Once a Thief*, we meet a number of characters who all have their own stories to tell. Here are some of the supporting cast members and where you would see them again.

Leland Yang-Joule is in BINARY HACKERS

A hacker, Leland is one of the founders of Binary Systems, Inc., a computer network security company based in Atlanta, Georgia, that is helpful to Helen Hu in *Once a Thief*. Leland appears again in the supporting cast of my Binary Hackers series and in *Never a Traitor* in the Defender Sweethearts series. All these prepare Leland for her own series in the future.

Binary Hackers
JanThompson.com/binary

Never a Traitor (Defender Sweethearts Book 1)
JanThompson.com/traitor

Camden La Salle is in LOVE YOU ALWAYS

A reinstated FBI special agent now working for the FBI Art Crime Team, Camden once worked for Helen at Hu Knows, Inc. He makes cameo appearances in *Know You More* (Savannah Sweethearts Book 1) and *Tell You Soon* (Savannah Sweethearts Book 2).

His own story is told in *Love You Always* in the Savannah Sweethearts series. In this novel, Camden returns to Savannah to work for his private investigator friend, Ming Wei. Ming assigns him to aid in the search for a missing woman, who turns out to be the sister of his former girlfriend. Will Camden get a second chance at love with Iris Delaney?

Love You Always (Savannah Sweethearts Book 6)
JanThompson.com/love

Sabine Hu-Wei is in TELL YOU SOON

A real estate agent, Sabine is Helen Hu's younger sister. She lives in Savannah, Georgia, with her husband, Private Investigator Ming Wei.

Sabine's love relationship with Ming begins in *Tell You Soon*. While Ming hunts for an international fugitive, he is also trying to get his personal finances in order. When he hires Sabine to sell his beach house on Tybee Island, his proximity to her puts her in harm's way in this friends-to-more romance with a side of suspense.

Tell You Soon (Savannah Sweethearts Book 2)
JanThompson.com/tell

Diego Flores is in KNOW YOU MORE

Diego is the pastor of Riverside Chapel, Helen Hu's home church. Diego appears in every book in the Savannah Sweethearts series, beginning with his own love story in book 1.

In *Know You More*, Diego is in love with his

best friend's sister, Heidi Wei, while he works hard at being the pastor he is called to be at Riverside Chapel in this friends-to-more coastal city and beach town romance.

Know You More (Savannah Sweethearts Book 1)
JanThompson.com/know

Sign up for my mailing list

If you like Christian romantic suspense, near-future technothrillers, coastal and beach romance, and romantic women's fiction, feel free to sign up for my mailing list. I'm writing more books for you to enjoy.

JanThompson.com/newsletter

Would you please post a review?

Thank you for reading *Once a Thief*. Would you be willing to write a review of this book? Reviews are very helpful to readers. You can find the links to book retailers for *Once a Thief* here:

Once a Thief (Protector Sweethearts Book 1)
JanThompson.com/thief

Sneak peek...

Continue reading for more information about the next book, *Once a Hero*, including a sneak peek of the prologue and chapter 1.

THE NEXT BOOK IS ONCE A HERO

PROTECTOR SWEETHEARTS BOOK 2

A former FBI agent and a treasure hunter must join forces to defeat a mutual enemy in a race to find treasures from the lost Amber Room.

Emerging from a deep undercover operation gone wrong, FBI Special Agent Jake Kessler finds himself suspended without pay and left out of the remaining hunt for the most notorious terrorist in the world. The only person who might be able to help him is a random stranger he meets in San Francisco, who wants something in return even when there is a price on her own head.

A relentless hunter...

They say that FBI Special Agent Jake Kessler doesn't follow orders, and that he deserves to be tortured and left to die on that sinking ship. Whatever. Jake is simply thankful he makes it out alive and in one piece, even though his cover is now blown.

The workaholic that he is, Jake doesn't know the meaning of suspension. On his own time, he goes to San Francisco to follow a tenuous lead. All he has to do is meet an informant who has news for him about the international criminal at large, Molyneux. Something goes wrong, and now Jake is fired from the bureau.

A reticent stranger...

Treasure hunter Beatrice Glynn is also at the restaurant to meet the same person, who would recognize Beatrice if not for her disguise. Beatrice's goal is to find the Amber Room before Molyneux does, thus fulfilling her deceased father's lifelong quest. Beatrice thinks she is very close. If she can only get a few more clues to the whereabouts of the Amber Room...

Beatrice does not want Jake to know who she is, but in the chaos at the restaurant, they meet face to face. Their goals intersect, and their hunting parties join forces.

A ruthless enemy...

Getting civilian into mortal danger when he doesn't have his badge isn't Jake's intention, but dying is the least of their worries when his archenemy finds them no matter where they go.

They can run, but they cannot hide from her. Why? How?

Their best bet to survive is to get ahead of their mutual enemy, who will remove everyone in the way toward finding the remainder of the lost original Amber Room. But how can Jake and Beatrice find something that no longer exists?

Once a Hero is book 2 in *USA Today* bestselling author Jan Thompson's **Protector Sweethearts** Christian Romantic Suspense series. *Once a Hero* follows the story of FBI Special Agent Jake Kessler, who first appears undercover in *Reach for Me* (Vacation Sweethearts Book 2), where the hunt for an international terrorist forms the undercurrent of that novel.

Once a Hero (Protector Sweethearts Book 2):
JanThompson.com/oncehero

Protector Sweethearts:
JanThompson.com/protector

To be notified when this book is released:
JanThompson.com/newsletter

Please keep reading for a preview of the prologue and chapters 1-2.

ONCE A HERO SNEAK PEEK (PROLOGUE & CHAPTER 1)

PROTECTOR SWEETHEARTS BOOK 2

Prologue

The sounds of his own bones cracking threw FBI Special Agent Jake Kessler into another blinding mental vortex so dark and deep that he couldn't hear his own screams, muffled under the oily, bloody rag they had stuffed into his mouth and tied around the back of his head.

A boot on his chest, pressing down at his rib cage and the internal organs inside.

Can't breathe!

Strong hands had held his head in an odd position, and if they had pulled him any farther back as he lay prone on the floor, still tied to that chair, Jake was sure his neck would snap—

But then it wouldn't matter anymore, would it, if he had died?

God, let me die...

"I told you it wasn't me!" Molyneux screamed into his ear again as she drew the blade of her dagger into his thigh, twisting and shredding his muscles.

The pain was so unbearable that Jake was going to pass out.

Help me, God!

Still, nothing happened.

It was ridiculous to consider how much pain he could tolerate, but here was his test.

Slowly, Molyneux withdrew her dagger.

Whoa. I'm still alive.

God must have something for me to do, yes?

How much could Jake do in his condition, in this place? He opened his one non-swollen eye to look around him in the dimly lit hole in the ground.

Ah, he had been on the other side of this equation once, interrogating suspects, albeit in a more civilized manner becoming of the twenty-first century. He would have extended more mercy to Molyneux's goons. Goons who were now pistol-whipping him again.

Thwack! Thwack!

Funny how it sounded at close range.

God, let me die...

How many times had Molyneux confessed to him, her prisoner? Yeah, she had repeated ad infinitum that she had not been guilty of the Vienna bombings.

Or Tel Aviv.

Or Rome.

Or Barcelona, for that matter.

Oh, and Paris.

The list had gone on and on.

Denials, all.

Tasting his own blood from his busted lips, Jake couldn't process everything the French-born woman had been saying, let alone believe that she was to be absolved of all those terrorist acts that had her thumbprints all over them.

Those had all been signature Molyneux moves.

Operating under the radar through highly secure virtual private networks that even the NSA had envied, Molyneux moved in the darkness of evil.

The first time Jake had met her, he was shocked to find her looking like an ordinary woman who might live down the street from his mother's house.

Big brown eyes, braided brown hair—like she was from small-town America somewhere.

It was hard for Jake to believe that this plain woman was behind the worst terrorist attacks in the western hemisphere of the world.

And it was even harder for him to believe that she was pushing fifty.

Maybe it's plastic—

A crackle of thunder rocked the room.

Rocked?

Are we on a boat?

Jake couldn't speak, but he could still hear, see, think.

He blinked, trying to recall how he got here. All he could remember was that he had been sitting in a coffee shop in Cannes, waiting for an informant, when something pricked his neck—

The next thing he knew, he had blacked out and woken up in this place.

He hadn't eaten since then.

He felt thirsty, but the oily rag in his mouth only made him gag.

Several peals of thunder rocked the room again.

A heavy door flung open. A tall, well-armed man entered and whispered in Molyneux's ear.

Without another word, she left with him.

And so did her goons.

The room listed. Jake's chair tilted over and slid all the way to a wall.

Now Jake was sure they were on a boat.

In a storm at sea.

In the Bay of Cannes, perhaps?

As if on cue, the sound of thunder boomed through the vessel.

The entire cabin rolled until Jake was looking up at the locked door.

He heard all sorts of metallic and oceanic noise, but what he saw scared him.

Water seeped in all around the supposedly heavy, sealed door...

Chapter 1

Six months later, Jake Kessler had no idea why Molyneux had chosen to confront him personally, out on a fishing boat in the Bay of Cannes in a thunderstorm, no less.

All he knew was that if his private investigator friend, Helen Hu, hadn't come to his rescue, he would have drowned at the bottom of the sea, leaving the hunt for Molyneux unfinished and someone else's problem.

However, he had lived to tell the tale—albeit through multiple surgeries later—and so, yeah, Molyneux was still his problem, although he had to regroup without a team.

Jake couldn't comprehend the sudden suspension without pay. For what, exactly? For almost dying in the hands of Molyneux?

The Bureau wasn't sympathetic to his life-and-death situation. All they cared was that their multi-million-dollar operation had ground to a screeching halt because Jake had blown his cover.

Unintentionally, he might add.

But nobody would listen.

The suspension stood.

Helen Hu had offered to pay him a stipend if he wanted to continue the operation against Molyneux.

Who wouldn't?

But first, Jake had to recover from his wounds. Staying in the Paris apartment rent-free with

Helen Hu and Reuben Costa while they were on their delayed honeymoon was weird, to say the least, but he mostly kept to himself in his space while they occupied the rest of the luxurious apartment.

In all his life, Jake had never met another couple working through their honeymoon.

Yet they had no choice. Molyneux had bombed Cannes one day after Jake was rescued. All that went into the report that caused Jake to get suspended.

If Jake hadn't gone off script and agreed to meet an informant in Cannes, perhaps the row of historic hotels could have been saved from the blaze.

In any case, Jake didn't get his meeting in Cannes either. Molyneux's people got to him first.

He thought the informant was dead until she contacted him two days ago.

Which was why Jake was in a transatlantic private jet now, heading for San Francisco.

This time, the informant had better show up.

Stretched out on the reclining leather seat, Jake rolled his head to one side to look out of the window. It was all dark.

He glanced at his watch. He'd arrive in San Francisco in two hours, drive half an hour to the twenty-four-hour restaurant—traffic should be light at two in the morning—and pray that the informant would show up.

At some point in time, the wild goose chase had to end.

"That all we got on Molyneux?" A voice broke his muse.

Private investigator Earl Young tossed the folder back on the table between them. The way the seats were configured in Helen's jet, Jake couldn't reach for the folder from his reclining position.

Jake glanced over his feet at the end of the recliner. On the other side of the table, Earl was sitting up, swiping his iPad.

"There has to be something more. She didn't become Molyneux the Doll overnight." Earl didn't look up. "What about family? Parents? Siblings? Spouses?"

"What you see is all we get." Jake pointed to the table. "Four years of work right there."

"And still no fingerprint, no DNA, no first names. For all we know, she might not exist."

"Few people know her real name." Jake crossed his feet. He wiggled his toes in his hiking socks.

The temperature in the cabin was warm, but once they get on the ground, he needed to dress warmly for the low fifties in the middle of the night.

Days in San Francisco were mild, but the informant wanted to meet under the cover of night.

"She has to have been born somewhere." Earl tapped his iPad. "Do we know if she has always been a French citizen?"

"You read my report from the Bay of Cannes incident," Jake said. "I looked into her eyes and I talked to her, and if I didn't know any better, I'd say she looked like a neighbor next door or down the street who probably owns a pair of gardening gloves. If she walked in the streets of Cannes or Paris or maybe even San Francisco, I might not be able to peg her as the world's top terrorist."

Earl nodded. "That's how she has hidden from the law for the last ten years."

"Or more."

"I'll dig into her past and see what I can unearth. How long are you going to be in the States?"

Jake shrugged. "I don't know. Frankly, just between you and me, I want to be done with this operation."

"Well, the Bureau thinks you already are." Earl leaned back and closed his eyes.

Jake had nothing to say about that. He was pulled into the operation when his FBI partner died in Vienna in the explosion. The man was celebrating his twentieth wedding anniversary with his beloved wife. The blast left his wife maimed.

After that tragedy, an opportunity came up for him to go on deep undercover in Molyneux's organization. Being single and unattached, Jake took up the multi-year operation.

His sole contact inside the FBI, Stella Evans, had been his only lifeline to the outside world as he navigated the sewers of Molyneux's operation for three years.

And yet, in all that time, Jake never could get up close and personal with Molyneux until that day in the boat.

Even before he had recovered from his wounds, Jake received the news about his suspension based on entirely frivolous reasons, including turning renegade and arranging a meeting with an informant without proper backups.

Jake supposed that made it all better and hid the fact that Molyneux's people could stab his neck with a needle under the noses of all the FBI agents in the coffee shop that day.

Someday he'd have enough evidence to get his paycheck back.

Meanwhile, he had to keep working on taking down Molyneux, even if the entire Bureau had given up on her. Jake was thankful that when the

FBI door slammed in his face, that God opened another door for him.

Helen said that Earl and Hugo were her most trusted investigators at Hu Knows, Inc. Hugo was still in Brussels and on another case. Earl had gone to Athens, Greece, for a company meeting with Helen Hu, who hadn't left Europe since her marriage to Reuben Costa.

Since Earl was taking their corporate jet back to Savannah, Helen had suggested that Jake fly home with him. Halfway over the Atlantic, Earl asked to be on the project. The airplane refueled in Atlanta, and off the duo went across the country.

Jake welcomed Earl's help. After all, he needed all the assistance he could get without involving any of his friends still in the Bureau.

Yes, he knew about the FBI mole. However, he didn't think it was going to affect this situation.

Would it?

Chapter 2

Beatrice Glynn blamed jet lag for keeping her awake at three in the morning on the west coast— six in the morning in Charleston, where she would have been just waking up to the first cup of coffee that her brother made for her every morning whenever she went to see him.

Instead here she was, waiting for the Ghost of Christmas Past to appear at the next table in the uncrowded brand new twenty-four-hour café overlooking San Francisco Bay.

Beatrice wondered how her brother was doing these couple of days she had been away, flying back and forth between Europe and North America. He had told her never to call whenever she was out and about, hunting for treasures connected to the Amber Room.

Her brother was even more paranoid than she.

Yeah, Benjamin was just as paranoid as Dad when he had been alive. Dad would still be alive had Molyneux not killed him a few years after Dad obtained asylum in the United States and ended up in the witness protection program as a single father of two kids.

Beatrice was eight years old when Dad died without a body to bury.

She found out later that Dad hadn't been a hero she had thought he was. While nurturing a career as a treasure hunter, in reality Dad was a thief and a partner in crime of Molyneux. Of course, it was all hearsay.

Truth be told, Beatrice hardly remembered the lost years. She was only five years old when she was whisked to the USA and told they would have new names. No longer the Wright family, they would henceforth be the Glynn family. Benjamin was ten, and his story about the event grew more intense and sinister over the years.

I can't blame him.

Beatrice suspected that if she had been ten years old watching her own father be executed, she could be traumatized the rest of her life too. In spite of their loving foster parents, the emotional trauma would remain.

No wonder Benjamin was a recluse now and hadn't left the house for as long as Beatrice could remember. He worked from home, had groceries delivered to him, and stayed away from public.

As for Beatrice, she had taken the opposite direction. Whether she favored her father or a mother she never knew was beside the matter. The point was that she realized she couldn't be hiding away in a mansion, however nice it was, forever.

Someone had to bring the fight back to Molyneux.

Both she and her brother lived with the fact that any day now, Molyneux would come after them to finish the job she started thirty years prior.

And when she came, Beatrice would be waiting for her.

In fact, rather than let Molyneux find her way to the Glynn siblings, Beatrice was determined to set a trap for the queen rat.

And it had everything to do with the Amber Room.

Ever since she graduated with a doctorate degree in history, with concentration in World War II, Beatrice had set her mind on a race to find the remaining panels of the lost Amber Room before Molyneux did. Then she could dangle the artifact in front of the terrorist and somehow deliver him to the authorities.

How exactly would she do that last part?

Well, she hadn't figured it out entirely yet although she'd get there soon.

First, she had to put the remaining puzzle together.

Her contact had notified her that the quarry had left France for San Francisco by way of Mexico. This was the same woman who had tried to meet the FBI Special Agent in Cannes some six months prior.

As if taunting death, Philomena Caddock seemed to be attempting to contact the agent again. Had she found the key to the music box that was supposed to be hidden in a forest somewhere?

And how did Philomena come upon such a crucial piece of information?

Had she gotten it from Dad back when she worked as a nanny and found her way into Dad's bedroom in England? They had carried on for several years before Mom found out about the affair, ending their already fractured marriage.

Being forever branded as the homewrecker wasn't enough for Philomena? Now she revealed herself to be a thief as well, stealing things from Dad that probably hadn't rightfully belonged to him.

No wonder Molyneux wanted her dead.

Everyone wanted Philomena dead.

Foot traffic was light at this hour of the night compared to six hours before when Beatrice and her team had eaten dinner in the back of a van going up and down Fisherman's Wharf. Raynelle Dryden and Kenichi were simply happy they weren't the ones showing their faces to citywide public security cameras placed all over San Francisco.

Sitting in the van monitoring the situation was a boring task. Yet Beatrice wouldn't have been a successful treasure hunter if not for those two. She kept giving them a raise every year, with bonuses at Christmas.

It had been Kenichi who had told Beatrice about the Crete discovery. One single panel from the Amber Room had been buried in a woman's crypt. When the panel was returned to the Russian curators of the Catherine Palace, Beatrice and Kenichi did some research that led them to an FBI mole who revealed that an agent named Jake Kessler had been deep undercover in Molyneux's organization.

The agent was hard to track. He was like a shadow in the night.

However, the wedding of his friend, private investigator Helen Hu, wasn't as secret. It was all over the news because Helen's mother had been convicted of an old crime, also related to the Amber Room.

One thing led to another, and Beatrice and her team had followed Helen Hu and her new husband, Reuben Costa, as they made their way to Paris, where they met up with FBI Special Agent Jake Kessler.

Kenichi and Raynelle tracked Helen and Reuben online, while Beatrice followed Kessler to Cannes. So did Molyneux.

Beatrice prayed that Molyneux had not followed Philomena to San Francisco.

Still gathering her weapons, Beatrice was not ready to fight Molyneux right now.

However, the meeting was tonight, like it or not.

Dressed as a server, Raynelle had done the work of sneaking into the busy café during its peak hours, and assigning Beatrice to the table next to Jake Kessler and Philomena, who had made a reservation under the name of Chisolm Wright—which had thrown Beatrice off for a moment.

Chisolm Wright had been Dad's real name when the family was still living in England. When they approved his asylum application, he came over to the States as Thomas Peterson. His son, Eugene, became Benjamin, and his daughter, Amber, became Amberlyn and then later, Beatrice after Dad died when they were yet again adopted by a wealthy family in Charleston.

While Dad was still alive, he forbade them all to speak of their adoptive mother. Beatrice often wondered what had happened to Imogen Wright, a woman of French descent studying in England and meeting her treasure hunter husband at Oxford.

To this day, no one knew where she had vanished to.

And now, after twenty-five years, someone had called on Dad's old name.

Why did Philomena ask the FBI agent to reserve a table for two under Chisolm Wright? The meeting had to be about Dad's dealings with Molyneux. How much did Philomena know?

Beatrice was there to find out.

Perhaps she might even discover what had happened to Mom. Had she died? Had Molyneux or Philomena killed her?

A wig and a face mask were all it took for Beatrice to subvert the facial recognition cameras outside and inside the café. In fact, it was a requirement all over the city to wear a mask—or face covering—to restaurants and public places, a new normal borne out of a recent virus pandemic.

Ironically, it was going to make it hard for Beatrice to recognize Philomena.

Except for the scar across her left eyebrow—a gift from Molyneux in Cannes. Beatrice remembered watching Philomena escape. They lost track of her after that.

However, she was back on a beautiful night in San Francisco.

A server came to refill Beatrice's glass of water.

She had been sitting alone for a while, playing

with her phone. Clearly Philomena and FBI agent were late.

How did Philomena elude the authorities for twenty-five years?

Well, how did Molyneux?

Why hadn't the two met and dealt with each other in all those years? More unsolved puzzles there.

Beatrice felt no pity for those two women. For one thing, Molyneux had killed so many people that she would never leave prison—if she made it into prison. Numerous government agencies in North America and Europe were after her.

The server returned. "Would you like something else, ma'am?"

"May I have the dessert menu?" Beatrice felt like she had to blend in. Most of the people in the café were eating something.

"Certainly, ma'am. I'll be right back."

At 3:28 a.m. there was still no sign of anyone.

Beatrice's shoulders began to hurt a little. Sore muscles here and there. She had slept poorly in the Gulfstream, besotted with worries about the project to take down Molyneux.

Once in San Francisco, she and her team had booked a hotel room and rented a work van. Then they ate meals in town, got takeouts, went to the gas station.

She had left an enormous trail for FBI Special Agent Jake Kessler.

To wit, if anything happened to her—should Molyneux decide to come after her—she had left enough footprints for Kessler to exonerate her or at least bring closure to her case in the event that it turned into a homicide.

She wouldn't put it past Molyneux to do whatever she could to be the first person to get to the rest of the Amber Room.

The server returned and Beatrice kept it simple with a slice of chocolate cake with ice cream on top. When it arrived, she nearly forgot what she was there to do.

"That looks delicious."

The voice was calm, friendly, and distinctly male.

Beatrice looked up, her fork in midair.

"Such a tiny slice." It was all she could think of to say.

Jake Kessler smiled.

A nice voice that went with a disarming smile.

They finally met, but Kessler would never know that she knew who he was long before today.

He had gotten a haircut since Cannes, though

that had been six months prior. Those scars on his forehead and left cheek were healing nicely.

Beatrice wanted to ask about his ribs, which Molyneux's men had broken, but that would give her away to both the FBI and to Molyneux.

She wasn't sure which one was worse.

Regardless, she was glad that he was still alive.

Her anonymous tip to Helen Hu's personal cell phone had been a knee-jerk reaction. Beatrice could not let a fellow human being die in the ocean when she knew where Molyneux had taken him. The sudden storm was something else. She was surprised that Molyneux had escaped in a helicopter before the fishing boat capsized.

Thank God Helen and her team had reached him in time.

Even though Kessler didn't know Beatrice, she had made him her insurance.

The man sat down without another word.

Just as well. Beatrice did not want to say anything that would give away who she was.

Quietly, she scanned the room. By a dark window, Raynelle was eating salad and reading a book. Presumably she had finished her work as a server in an earlier shift. A former CIA operative, Raynelle Dryden was a coup for Beatrice.

Officially, Raynelle was her bodyguard due to

some previous death threats. Unofficially, Raynelle's job was to assist Beatrice in finding the rest of the lost Amber Room. That was Kenichi's job too.

Around them, several other tables were occupied, but the people generally looked like customers.

The stage was set.

All they needed now was the woman of the hour to make a grand entrance.

Once a Hero (Protector Sweethearts Book 2): JanThompson.com/oncehero

Protector Sweethearts: JanThompson.com/protector

Sign up for book news from Jan Thompson: JanThompson.com/newsletter

ACKNOWLEDGMENTS

Many thanks to my Georgia Press publishing team for keeping up with my busy schedule for this book.

My copyeditors, Dori Harrell and Lesley McDaniel, are tireless and timely. Thank you, ladies.

With sharp eyes from the Lord, Lenda Selph proofread this book, together with Judy DeVries and Noah Thompson.

Regarding FBI procedural information, I thank private investigator and former FBI agent Steven Kerry Brown for answering my fact-checking questions.

I also thank my husband and our son for their constant support and encouragement.

And I'll always remember my dear mother and late father for instilling in me the love to read and write at a very early age.

Most of all, I am eternally thankful to my Lord and Savior, Jesus Christ, who died on the cross to save me from my sins and rose again from the grave to give me eternal life. Without Him, I can write nothing (John 15:5).

Joyfully in Jesus,
Jan Thompson
John 3:16

BOOKS BY JAN THOMPSON

Christian Beach and Island Romance

Seaside Chapel (7 Books)
JanThompson.com/seaside
Journeys of Love through Life's Ups & Downs

Christian Coastal Romance in the South

Savannah Sweethearts (12 Books)
JanThompson.com/savannah

Christian Travel Romance

Vacation Sweethearts (8 Books)
JanThompson.com/vacation

Christian Christmas Romance in the City

Midtown Christmas (4 Books)
JanThompson.com/christmas

Christian Christmas Romance on the Coast

Christmas Sweethearts (3 Books)
JanThompson.com/christmastown

International Christian Romantic Suspense

Protector Sweethearts (6 Books)
JanThompson.com/protector
Treasures Lost and Found

Defender Sweethearts (6 Books)
JanThompson.com/defender
Defending the Defenseless Worldwide

Near-Future Technothrillers with Christian
Romance

Binary Hackers (4 Books)
    JanThompson.com/binary
    Cyberthrillers

Christian Suspense in Between Series

Guardian Sweethearts (2 Books)
    JanThompson.com/guardian

Subscribe to Jan Thompson's mailing list:
JanThompson.com/newsletter

SEASIDE CHAPEL

Welcome to *USA Today* bestselling author Jan Thompson's Seaside Chapel Christian beach romance series. These novels are set on real-life St. Simon's Island, Georgia—a beach town where history is all around and the future is a moment away—and the neighboring fictitious Seaside Island, where the rich and famous live.

Savor the small-town atmosphere and the warm southern beaches of St. Simon's Island and the idyllic Golden Isles along the Atlantic Ocean. Enjoy the music of the orchestra and hymns of the church, and hang out with our Christian friends who attend Seaside Chapel, a little church by the sea known for its beach weddings and fair share of love and life.

As these Christians grow in their knowledge and understanding of God, they are tested in their spiritual maturity, their love lives, and their relationships with others. Share their heartaches and healing, and cheer them on as they celebrate faith, family, and friends.

JanThompson.com/seaside

- Book 0 (Prequel): *His Surprise Proposal*
- Book 1: *His Longing Heart*
- Book 2: *His Wake-Up Call*
- Book 3: *His Morning Kiss*
- Book 4: *His Quiet Serenade*
- Book 5: *His Waiting Love*
- Book 6: *His Beach Retreat*

SAVANNAH SWEETHEARTS

Welcome to the new south! From *USA Today* bestselling author Jan Thompson come these clean and wholesome, sweet and inspirational Christian romances set on the romantic beaches of Tybee Island and in the coastal town of Savannah, Georgia. Meet a group of multiracial and multiethnic churchgoing Christians who love the Lord, work hard in their careers, and seek God's will for their love lives. Against a backdrop of ocean, sand, and sun, these inspirational romances showcase aspects of the human need for God and for one another. Have some tea, settle in a comfortable reading chair, and enjoy these sweet celebrations of faith, hope, and love in Jesus Christ.

JanThompson.com/savannah

- Book 1: *Ask You Later* (Artist Romance)
- Book 2: *Know You More* (Multiracial Romance)
- Book 3: *Tell You Soon* (Asian-American Romance with Suspense)
- Book 4: *Draw You Near* (International Romance)
- Book 5: *Cherish You So* (Wheelchair Billionaire Romance)
- Book 6: *Walk You There* (Old-Meets-New Tour Guide Romance)
- Book 7: *Love You Always* (Romance with Suspense)
- Book 8: *Kiss You Now* (Multiracial Romance)
- Book 9: *Find You Again* (Multiracial Romance)
- Book 10: *Wish You Joy* (Christmas-Themed Romance)
- Book 11: *Call You Home* (Deaf Chef Romance)
- Book 12: *Let You Go* (Asian-American Romance with Suspense)

VACATION SWEETHEARTS

Travel with our friends from Savannah, Georgia, to the coast and to the mountains. Cheer them on as they celebrate the immeasurable grace and undeserved mercy of God through Jesus Christ.

The Vacation Sweethearts novels are a spin-off of Jan's Savannah Sweethearts series, and fans will recognize familiar faces from Riverside Chapel, a church in the coastal city of Savannah, Georgia. In fact, we might even visit the beach town of Tybee Island from time to time to visit old friends and beloved families...

JanThompson.com/vacation

- Book 0 (Prequel): *Time for Me*
- Book 1: *Smile for Me* (Beach Romance in the Bahamas)
- Book 2: *Reach for Me* (Romance with Suspense in the Smoky Mountains)
- Book 3: *Wait for Me* (Romance with Suspense on a Cruise Ship)
- Book 4: *Look for Me* (Romance with Suspense in a Florida Beach Town)
- Book 5: *Pray for Me* (International Romance in the City of Atlanta)
- Book 6: *Care for Me* (Small Mountain Town Romance)
- Book 7: *Cheer for Me* (International Romance)

Read *Time for Me* (Prequel) for free:
JanThompson.com/time-free

CHRISTMAS SWEETHEARTS

Welcome to Christmastown, that holiday decorating company that is now run by Cyrus Theroux and his lovely wife, Amy Untermeyer-Theroux. Their story is first told in Wish You Joy (Savannah Sweethearts Book 10), the prequel to this Christmas Sweethearts series.

When this holiday romance series begins, Amy's Christmas Tree Farm and Christmastown have merged their daily operations at their Savannah headquarters.

JanThompson.com/christmastown

CHRISTMAS SWEETHEARTS

- Book 1: *Wish You Faith*
- Book 2: *Wish You Hope*
- Book 3: *Wish You Peace*

MIDTOWN CHRISTMAS

Big city romance, small town feel. Four Christian couples minister at Midtown Chapel in metro Atlanta, and Midtown Village, the community of tiny homes for needy families. From November to January every year, this place turns into a Christmas Village for a small-town feel right there in the metropolis of Atlanta, Georgia.

JanThompson.com/christmas

- Book 1: *Let Me Hold You* (Levi Theroux and Maggie Jacobs from *Pray for Me*)

- Book 2: *Let Me Adore You* (Erika Song from *Look for Me* and Hiroki Yamada from *Walk You There*)
- Book 3: *Let Me Honor You* (Forsythia McDevitt from *Call You Home* and Owen Grayson from *Find You Again*)
- Book 4: *Let Me Love You* (Leila Patel from *Find You Again*)

PROTECTOR SWEETHEARTS

Private investigator Helen Hu and her associates specialize in searching for missing persons and hunting for lost treasures. Join them in their adventure suspense around the world in *USA Today* bestselling author Jan Thompson's Protector Sweethearts, a series of Christian Romantic Suspense with a side of mystery.

Protector Sweethearts is a spin-off of Savannah Sweethearts and Vacation Sweethearts.

JanThompson.com/protector

- Book 1: *Once a Thief*

- Book 2: *Once a Hero*
- Book 3: *Once a Spy*
- Book 4: *Twice a Fighter*
- Book 5: *Twice a Convict*
- Book 6: *Twice a Soldier*

DEFENDER SWEETHEARTS

Defender Sweethearts is a sister series to the Protector Sweethearts Christian romantic suspense collection. While the heroes in Protector Sweethearts search for lost treasures and lost people, the Defender Sweethearts novels focus on protecting the helpless and hopeless. The main characters in Defender Sweethearts come from the supporting cast in Protector Sweethearts.

JanThompson.com/defender

- Book 1: *Never a Traitor*

- Book 2: *Never a Hostage*
- Book 3: *Never a Fugitive*
- Book 4: *Always a Maverick*
- Book 5: *Always a Champion*
- Book 6: *Always a Guardian*

BINARY HACKERS

Like more suspense with your Christian romance? Like to read suspense thrillers? If you're looking for clean near-future romantic suspense without compromising the Christian faith, these books are for you.

From *USA Today* bestselling author Jan Thompson come these inspirational near-future cyberthrillers combining technothriller and romance, starting with Binary Hackers that feature computer specialists living at the edge of cyberspace, where they have to juggle being law-abiding truth-telling Christians while carrying out their assignments by any and all means possible.

The Binary Hackers series is set in the same story world as Jan's other books, and characters from the other series may make cameo appearances in this series and vice versa.

JanThompson.com/binary

- Book 1: *Zero Sum*
- Book 2: *Zero Day*
- Book 3: *Zero Out*
- Book 4: *Zero Trust*

ABOUT JAN THOMPSON

USA Today bestselling author Jan Thompson writes clean and wholesome multiethnic contemporary Christian romance with elements of women's fiction, Christian romantic suspense with an air of mystery, and inspirational international thrillers with threads of sweet Christian romance.

Raised on a tropical island in the eastern hemisphere, Jan now lives and writes in the western hemisphere. Her international background gives her a unique multicultural and multiracial perspective to her novels and books.

After earning a Bachelor of Science degree in Computer Science, Jan worked as a database programmer and information technology consultant for many years before transitioning from writing software to her lifelong dream job of writing fiction.

Jan's books are for readers who love inspiring stories of faith, hope, and love in Jesus Christ.

~

Find out more about Jan Thompson:
JanThompson.com

Subscribe to Jan's book news mailing list:
JanThompson.com/newsletter

For God so loved the world
that He gave His only begotten Son,
that whoever believes in Him
should not perish but have everlasting life.
—John 3:16